Rendell, Ruth
Blood lines   23.00
                                    6/96

BLOOD
LINES

RUTH RENDELL

BLOOD LINES

Long and Short Stories

CROWN PUBLISHERS, INC.

NEW YORK

Ren

The following stories were originally published in *Ellery Queen:* "Shreds and Slivers" (November 1994), "Unacceptable Levels" (March 1995), "In All Honesty" (November 1995), "Burning End" (December 1995), "Lizzie's Lover" (December 1995), "The Carer" (January 1996), "Clothes" (February 1996), and "Expectations" (March 1996). "The Strawberry Tree" was originally published in *Unguarded Hours,* published by Pandora Books in 1990.

Published by Crown Publishers, Inc., 201 East 50th Street, New York, New York 10022. Member of the Crown Publishing Group.

Random House, Inc. New York, Toronto, London, Sydney, Auckland

CROWN is a trademark of Crown Publishers, Inc.

Originally published in Great Britain by Random House UK in 1996.

Printed in the United States of America

Design by Leonard Henderson

Library of Congress Cataloging-in-Publication Data
Rendell, Ruth
    Blood lines / Ruth Rendell.—1st ed.
    1. Detective and mystery stories, English.   I. Title.
    PR6068.E63B56   1996
    823'.914—dc20   96-852

ISBN 0-517-70323-8

10 9 8 7 6 5 4 3 2 1

First American Edition

For Don

Contents

BLOOD LINES

———————

"I think you know who killed your stepfather," said Wexford.

It was a throwaway line, uttered on parting and over his shoulder as he reached the door. A swift exit was, however, impossible. The moment he got up he had not to duck his head merely but bend himself almost double. The girl he spoke to was a small woman, the boyfriend she lived with no more than five feet six. Life in the caravan, he thought, would otherwise have been insupportable.

Stuck in the doorway, he said when she made no reply, "You won't mind if I come back in a day or two and we'll have another talk."

"All the same if I do, isn't it?"

"You don't have to talk to me, Miss Heddon. It's open to you to say no." It would all have been more dignified if he could have stood up and faced her, but Wexford wasn't much concerned with dignity. He spoke rather gravely but with gentleness. "But if you've no objection we'll continue this conversation on Monday. I've a feeling you know a lot more than you've told me."

She said it, one of those phrases that invariably means its opposite. "I don't know what you're talking about."

"That's unworthy of someone of your intelligence," he said, and he meant it.

He opened the door and climbed out. Climbing, half crouched, was the only way. It was with relief that he put his feet on the ground, got his head clear, and straightened himself up to his full height. She had followed him and stood there, holding the door, a pretty young woman of twenty who looked even younger than her age because her blond hair was waist-length and her white blouse schoolgirlish.

"Monday, then," Wexford said. "Shall we say three-ish?"

"Suit yourself." With one of her flashes of humor, she said, "You must feel like a Rottweiler in a rabbit hutch in here."

He smiled. "You may be right. It's true my bite is worse than my bark."

Possibly digesting this, she closed the door without another word. He picked his way back to the car where Donaldson waited at the wheel. A path of cinders made a just-usable track across the corner of a muddy field. In the cold haze the shape of a cottage converted from a railway carriage could just be seen against a gray tangle of wilderness. Two inches of rain had fallen in the week since Tom Peterlee's death, and the sky of massive gray cumulus was loaded with more.

"We live in a caravan culture, Steve," he said to Donaldson. "As homes, I mean, not mobile tents. You can see two more over there—traveling farmworkers, I imagine. The one on the corner patch up here has been there at least two years and to my knowledge is home to four people, a dog, and a hamster."

"It wouldn't suit me, sir. Though, mind you, I'd have gone down on my bended knees in gratitude for a caravan when the wife and me were first married and living with her mum."

Wexford nodded, invisibly, from the back. "Go by way of Feverel's, will you? I don't want to stop, just take a look."

The Kenhurst road headed from the south for Edenwick and Kingsmarkham. Rain began to spit against the windshield as they came to the outskirts of Edenwick and its half-mile-long village street. After the houses ended, Feverel's buildings appeared as the car rounded a looplike bend in the road.

The farm shop remained closed, though a wooden board offering for sale apples, pears, plums, and walnuts for pickling still stood by the gate. Wexford told Donaldson to stop the car and park for a few moments. Let Heather Peterlee see him. That sort of thing did no harm. He looked, for the dozenth time, at the shack that had been a shop, the huddle of wooden buildings, the house itself, and the inevitable caravan.

"She'll have a job selling it, sir," said Donaldson as if reading his mind. "People won't much fancy the idea."

"The murder took place in the kitchen," Wexford said rather sharply, "not in that thing."

"It's all one to some," Donaldson said cryptically.

The house was a Victorian building, rendered in a pale stone color that the rain had turned to khaki, an uncompromising cheerless place with a window on either side of the front door that was plumb in the center and three windows above. No porch, balcony, or even trellis broke the monotony of its facade. The shallow roof was of dull-gray slate. Some ten yards of bleak ground, part gravel and part scrubby grass, separated the house from the shop. In between and a little distance behind, the caravan stood on a concrete slab, and beyond it stretched away the market gardens, looking from here no more than acres of cabbages. The only trees were the walnuts, still in leaf but the leaves tired and brown.

The shop, its double doors closed and padlocked, its windows boarded up, the display stalls that stood outside it gone, seemed a dilapidated hut. A sheet of the corrugated iron that roofed it had come loose and clanged up and down rhythmically in the increasing wind. It was a dreary place. No visitor would have difficulty in believing a man had been clubbed to death there. Wexford remembered, with distaste, the little crowds that had gathered outside this gate during the previous week, standing and watching, or sitting in the line of cars, some of them waiting for hours, staring at the house, hoping for happenings. Some of them recalling, no doubt, how a matter of days ago they had driven in for half a hundredweight of Maris Bards, a couple of pounds of Coxes, and one of Heather Peterlee's apple pies from the freezer.

As Donaldson started the engine a dog came out from the back of the house and began barking inside the gate. It was a black spaniel, but not of so mild a nature as is usually found in the breed. Wexford had felt its teeth through his jacket sleeve, though blood had not been drawn.

"That the dog, is it, sir?"

They all knew the story, even those only remotely involved. Wexford confirmed that this indeed was the dog, this was Scamp. The poor creature had recovered the voice it lost, giving continual tongue at the voyeurs until strain on its vocal cords struck it dumb.

4

Wexford spared a glance for the neighbors, if a house fifty yards of field and copse away can be called neighboring. Joseph Peterlee had a plant hire business and a customer was in the act of returning a mechanical digger with what looked like half a ton of the local chalky loam adhering to its giant wheels. In conversation with her husband and the digger driver on the concrete entrance, an area much cracked, pitted, and now puddled, was Mrs. Monica Peterlee in her unvarying uniform of rubber boots and floral crossover overall, holding over herself a green umbrella. And those are the characters in this drama, he thought, with the exception of one who (to paraphrase Kipling) has gone to the husband of her bosom the same as she ought to go, and one who has gone heaven only knows where.

Why was he so sure Arlene Heddon had the answer? Mike Burden, his second-in-command at Kingsmarkham CID, said with contempt that at any rate she was more attractive than the wife and the widow. With his usual distaste for those whose lives failed to approximate fairly closely his own, he spoke scathingly of "the Peterlee girl" as if having no job and no proper roof over one's head directly conduced to homicide.

"Her name," Wexford said rather dourly, "is Heddon. It was her father's name. Heather Peterlee, if you remember, was a Mrs. Heddon before she remarried." He added, wondering as he did so why he bothered to indulge Burden's absurd prejudices, "a widow, incidentally."

Quick as a flash, Burden came back with, "What did her first husband die of?"

"Oh God, Mike, some bone disease. We went into all that. But back to Arlene Heddon. She's a very intelligent young woman, you know."

"No, I don't know. You must be joking. Intelligent girls don't live on benefit in caravans with unemployed welders."

"What a snob you are."

"*Married* welders. I'm not just a snob, I'm a moralist. Intelligent girls do well at school, go on to further education, get suitable well-paid jobs, and buy themselves homes on mortgages."

"Somehow and somewhere along the line Arlene Heddon missed out on that. In any case, I didn't say she was academically inclined. She's sharp, she's clever, she's got a good brain."

"And her mother, the two-times widow, is she the genius Arlene inherited her IQ from?"

This was neither the time nor the place to be discussing the murder, Wexford's house on a Saturday evening, but Burden had come around for a drink and whatever the topic of conversation, things had a way of coming back to the Peterlees. They came back to the extent of Wexford's suggesting they go over the sequence of events again. Dora, his wife, was present, but sitting on the window seat, reading tranquilly. For once, he didn't suggest he and Burden go somewhere private.

"You can set me right on the details," Wexford began, "but I think you'll agree it was broadly like this. On Thursday, October tenth, Heather Peterlee opened the farm shop at Feverel's as usual at nine A.M. They had on sale their own produce and other more exotic vegetables and fruit they bought in. Heather had her sister-in-law Mrs. Monica Peterlee to help her, again as usual. Heather's husband, Tom, was working outside, and at lunchtime he brought up to the shop by tractor the vegetables he had lifted and picked during the morning.

"They ate their midday meal in the shop, keeping it open, and at three or thereabouts Joseph Peterlee arrived in his car to fetch his wife and take her shopping in Kingsmarkham. Tom and Heather served in the shop until closing time at five, when they returned to the house and Heather began preparing a meal. Tom had brought in the shop's takings with him, which he intended to put in the safe, but in the meantime he left the notes on the kitchen dresser that faces the outside door. The sum was about three hundred and sixty pounds. He put the money on the dresser shelf and placed on top of it his camera in its case, presumably to stop it blowing about when the door was opened. He then went to the caravan to discuss some matter of business with Carol Fox, who had been living there since the summer. In fact, the matter of business was the question of raising the rent she paid."

"Tom Peterlee wasn't killed for three hundred and sixty pounds," said Burden.

"No, but various people would like us to think he was. It's a problem even guessing why he was killed. Everyone seems to have liked him. We have had . . ." Wexford hesitated, " 'golden opinions from all sorts of people.' He was something of a paragon by all accounts, an ideal husband, good, kind, undeniably handsome. He was even handsome on the mortuary slab—forgive me, Dora.

"But I'll go on. They ate their meal at five-thirty. During the course of it, according to her statement, Tom said to his wife that they had fixed up the matter of the rent amicably. Carol wanted to stay on and understood the rent she was paying was inadequate—"

Dora interrupted him. "Is that the woman who'd left her husband, and Heather Peterlee said she could have their

7

caravan because she'd nowhere to live?"

"A friend of Heather's from way back, apparently. According to Heather, she told Tom she'd be around in an hour to accompany her on a dog walk. Heather always took the dog out after supper and Carol had got into the habit of going with her. Heather washed up their dishes and Tom dried. As I've said, he was an ideal husband. At some point he went out to the woodshed and fetched in a basket of logs to feed the wood-burning stoves, of which there was one in the kitchen and another in the living room.

"Carol knocked on the door and came into the kitchen at twenty past six. It wasn't raining but it looked like rain, and Carol was wearing only a cardigan. Heather suggested she put on one of the rainproof jackets of which there were several hanging behind the back door, and Carol took a fawn-colored one."

"Strange, wasn't it," Burden put in, "that she didn't fetch a coat of her own from the caravan? Especially a woman like that. Very conscious of her appearance, I'd say. But perhaps she wouldn't care, out on her own with another woman. It was a dull evening and they weren't likely to meet anyone."

Dora gave him a look, enigmatic, half smiling, but said nothing. Her husband went on:

"If you remember, when the caravan was searched as the house was, the fact was remarked on that Carol Fox had no raincoat among her clothes. She has said, and Heather has confirmed it, that she always used one of Heather's. They took the dog and went for a walk through Feverel's land, across the meadows by the public footpath, and down to the river. It was sometime between six-twenty and six-thirty that they left. It was still light and would be for another half hour. What Tom did in their absence we don't know and probably never shall know, except that putting that money into the safe wasn't among his activities.

"At about ten to seven Arlene Heddon arrived at Feverel's, brought in her boyfriend's van." Wexford raised an eyebrow at Burden. "The unemployed, married welder, Gary Wyatt.

"Arlene and Gary have no phone and Arlene got the message from Grandma, on whose land she lives. She's not really her grandmother, of course, but she calls her Grandma."

"The old witch," said Dora. "That's what people call her. She's well-known."

"I don't think she's as old as she looks, and she's definitely not a witch, though she cultivates that appearance. To be the mother of Joseph and Tom she need be no more than sixty-five, and I daresay she's not. The message Arlene got from Mrs. Peterlee Senior was that Mum had finished her jumper and if she wanted it for the Friday, could she come and pick it up? The time suggested was about eight. Grandma said she'd drive Arlene herself on account of she was going to her Conservative Association meeting in Kingsmarkham—I kid you not, Dora—but she said no, Gary and she would still be eating their tea. Gary would take her in the van a bit later on.

"In fact, Gary wanted to go out at half past six. He dropped her off at Feverel's, thus getting her there more than an hour earlier than her mother had suggested, and went on to have a drink with his pals in the Red Rose at Edenwick. Not that anyone has confirmed this. Neither the licensee nor the girl behind the bar remembers his being there, which is in direct contrast to the evidence of the old witch's witnesses. Strange as her presence there might seem, every Tory in Kingsmarkham seems to remember her in the 'Seminar Room' of the Olive and Dove Hotel that night. Not until seven-thirty, however, when the meeting started. Where had she been in that lost hour and a half?

"Gary promised to come back for Arlene in an hour. Arlene went round the back of the house and entered by the kitchen door, which was unlocked. As a daughter of the house, she didn't knock or call out, but walked straight in.

"There, in the kitchen, on the floor, she found the body of her stepfather, Tom Peterlee, lying face-downwards, with a wound in the back of the head. She knelt down and touched his face. It was still faintly warm. She knew there was a phone in the sitting room, but, fearing whoever had done this might still be in the house, she didn't go in there but ran back outside in the hope Gary had not yet gone. When she saw that he had she ran the hundred yards or so to Mr. and Mrs. Joe Peterlee's, where she used their phone and dialed 999.

"Joe Peterlee was out, according to his wife. Arlene—all this is Arlene's evidence, partly confirmed by Monica Peterlee—Arlene asked her to come back with her and wait for the police, but she said she was too frightened to do that, so Arlene went back alone. Within a very few minutes—it was now five past seven—her mother and Carol Fox returned from their walk with the dog. She was waiting for them outside the back door.

"She prepared them for what they would see and Heather cried out, pushed open the door, and rushed into the kitchen. She threw herself on the body, and when Arlene and Carol pulled her off and lifted her up, she began banging her head and face against the kitchen wall."

Burden nodded. "These two—what do we call them? hysterical acts? manifestations of grief?—account for the blood on the front of her jacket and the extensive bruising to her face. Or at least are possible explanations for them."

"The police came and everyone was questioned on the spot. Of course, no one had seen any suspicious characters hanging about Feverel's. No one ever has. Joe Peterlee has never been able to give a satisfactory account of his movements between six-twenty and six-fifty. Nor have Gary Wyatt and Grandma Peterlee.

"The money was gone. There was no weapon. No prints other than those of Tom, Heather, Carol Fox, and Arlene were found in the house. The pathologist says Tom died between six-fifteen and seven-fifteen, a time which can be much narrowed down if Arlene is to be believed. Remember, she says he felt warm when she touched him at six-fifty.

"I think she's lying. I think she's lying all along the line, she's protecting someone, and that's why I'm going to keep on talking to her until I find out who. Grandma or her boyfriend or her uncle Joe—or her mother."

Dora wrinkled up her nose. "Isn't it a bit distasteful, Reg, getting a girl to betray her own mother? It's like the KGB."

"And we know what happened to them," said Burden.

Wexford smiled. "I may only be getting her to betray her step-aunt by marriage, or isn't that allowed, either?"

Burden left them at about ten to ten. He was on foot, for he and Wexford lived less than a mile apart and walking was a preferable exercise to the kinds his wife suggested, riding a stationary bike or stomping up and down on a treadmill. His route home was to take him past the big new shopping mall, the York Crest Centre. He deplored the name and the

11

place, all a far cry from what Kingsmarkham had been when first he came there.

Then there was life in the town at night, people entering or emerging from pubs and restaurants, cinema visitors, walkers strolling, in those days before the ubiquitous car. Television, the effects of recession, and the fear of street violence had all combined to keep the townsfolk indoors and the place was deserted. It was silent, empty, but brightly lit, and therefore slightly uncanny.

His footfalls made a faint hollow echo, and he saw his solitary figure reflected in gleaming shop windows. Not a soul passed him as he entered York Street, not a single being waited on a corner or at the bus stop. He turned into the alley that ran along the side of the York Crest Centre, to cut a furlong or so off his journey. Does anyone know what a furlong is these days? thought old-fashioned, nostalgic Burden.

Into his silent speculation burst the raiders.

It took him about thirty seconds to realize what this was. He had seen it on television but thought it confined to the north. A ram raid. That was what someone had named this kind of heist. The Land Rover first, turning on the paved court, reversing at the highest speed it could make into the huge glass double doors that shut off the center by night. The noise of crashing glass was enormous, like a bomb.

It vanished inside, followed by two cars—a Volvo and a Volvo Estate—rattling over the broken glass, the wreckage of the doors. He didn't wait to see what happened. He had his cell phone in his hand and switched on before the second car's taillights had disappeared. "No Service" came up on its screen and "No Service" when he shook it and pulled the aerial out. It had gone wrong. Never before had that happened, but it had to happen tonight when he was in the right place at the right time.

Burden raced down the alley to the phones on the post office wall, four of them under plastic hoods. The first he tried had been vandalized; the second worked. If he could get them there within five minutes, within ten even . . . He pounded back, remembered it would be advisable not to be heard, and crept the rest of the way. They were leaving, the Land Rover—stolen, of course—with all its glass shattered, the two Volvos hard on its rear, and were gone God knew where by the time the Mid-Sussex Constabulary cars arrived.

❑   ❑   ❑

The purpose of the raid had been to remove as much electronic equipment as the thieves could lift in five minutes from Nixon's in the center. It had been a tremendous haul and had probably taken twelve men to accomplish it.

The phone on the post office wall was repaired and on the following day vandalized again along with all the others in the row. That was on a Monday, the date of Wexford's second conversation with Arlene Heddon. He went along to the caravan on old Mrs. Peterlee's land in the late afternoon. Arlene sometimes had a cleaning job, but she was always in during the afternoons. He tapped on the door and she called out to him to come in.

The television was on and she was watching, lounging on the seat that ran the length of the opposite wall. She looked so relaxed, even somnolent, that Wexford thought she would switch off by means of the channel changer, which lay on top of the partition that divided the living room/bedroom from the kitchen, but she got up and pressed the switch. They faced each other, and this time she seemed anxious to talk. He began to take her through a series of new inquiries and all the old ones.

He noticed then that what she said differed very slightly from what she had said the first time, if in minor details. Her mother had not thrown herself on the body but knelt down and cradled the dead man's head in her arms. It was on one of the counters, not against the wall, that she had beaten her head.

The dog had howled at the sight of its dead master. The first time she said she thought she had heard a noise upstairs when she first arrived. This time she said she denied it, all had been silent. She had not noticed if the money was there or not when she first arrived. Now she said the money was there with the camera on top of the notes. When she came back from making her phone call she had not gone back into the house but had waited outside for her mother to return. That was what she said the first time. Now she said she had gone briefly into the kitchen once more. The camera was there but the money gone.

Wexford pointed out these discrepancies in a casual way. She made no comment. He asked, with apparent indifference, "Just as a matter of interest, how did you know your mother was out with the dog?"

"The dog wasn't there and she wasn't."

"You were afraid to use the phone in the house in case your stepfather's killer might still be there. You never considered the possibility that your mother might have been dead in some other part of the house? That Carol Fox might have taken the dog out on her own, as perhaps she sometimes did?"

"I didn't know Carol very well," said Arlene Heddon.

It was hardly an answer. "But she was a close friend of your mother's, an old friend, wasn't she? You might say your mother offered her sanctuary when she left her husband. That's the action of a close friend, isn't it?"

"I haven't lived at home since I was seventeen. I don't know all the friends my mother's got. I didn't know whether Carol took the dog out or what. Tom sometimes took him out and my mother did. I never heard of Carol going with my mother, but I wouldn't. I wasn't interested in Carol."

"Yet you waited for them both to come back from their walk, Miss Heddon."

"I waited for my mother," she said.

Wexford left her, promising to come back for another talk on Thursday. Grandma was nowhere to be seen, but as he approached his car hers swept in, bumping over the rough ground, lurching through a trough or two, skidding with a scream of brakes on the ice, and, describing a swift half-circle around the railway carriage, juddering to a stop. Florrie Peterlee, pushing seventy and looking eighty, drove like an eighteen-year-old madman at the wheel of his first jalopy.

She gave the impression of clawing her way out. Her white hair was as long and straight as Arlene's, and she was always dressed in trailing black that sometimes had a curiously fashionable look. On a teenager it would have been trendy. She had a hooky nose and prominent chin, bright black eyes. But Wexford couldn't offhand think of anyone he knew who so intensely seemed to enjoy herself as Mrs. Peterlee Senior. Some of her pleasure derived from her indifference to what people thought of her, apart of course from her need to make them see her as a witch, some from her enduring good health and zest for life. So far she had shown no grief whatever at the death of her son.

"You're too old for her," said the old witch.

"Too old for what?" said Wexford, refusing to be outfaced.

"Ooh, hark at him! That's a nice question to ask a senior citizen. Mind I don't put a spell on you. Why don't you leave her alone, poor lamb."

"She's going to tell me who killed your son Tom."

"Get away. She don't know. Maybe I did." She stared at him with a bold defiance. "I all but killed his dad once. I said, you've knocked me about once too often, Arthur Peterlee, and I picked up the kitchen knife and come at him with it. I won't say he never touched me again, human nature never worked that way, but he dropped dead with his heart soon after, poor old sod. I was so glad to see the back of him, I danced on his grave. People say that, I know, it's just a way of talking, but me, I really did it. Went up the cemetery with a half-bottle of gin and danced on the bugger's grave."

Wexford could see her, hair flying, black draperies blowing, the bottle in one hand, her wrinkled face dabbled with gin, dancing under the rugged ilexes and the yew tree's shade. He put up his eyebrows. Before she had more chances to shock him, or try to, he asked her if she had thought any more about telling him where she had been in that lost hour on the evening of her son's death.

"You'd be surprised."

She said it, not as a figure of speech, but in the genuine belief she could astonish him. He had no doubt she could. She grinned, showing even white teeth, not dentures. The sudden thought came to him that if she had a good bath, put her copious hair up, and dressed in something more appropriate for a rural matriarch, she might look rather wonderful. He wasn't too worried about her alibi or lack of one, for he doubted if she had the strength to wield the "blunt instrument" that had killed Tom Peterlee.

He was very certain he knew what that instrument was and what had become of it. Arriving at Feverel's within the hour, he had seen the wood splinters in Tom Peterlee's head wound before the pathologist arrived. With a sinking heart he had taken in the implications of a basket full of logs just inside the back door and the big wood-burning enclosed stove in an embrasure of the wall facing the door into the house. They would never find the weapon. Without being able to prove it, he knew from the first that it had been an iron-hard log of oak, maybe a foot long and three or four inches in diameter, a log used to strike again and again, then pushed in among the blazing embers in that stove.

He had even looked. The stove had been allowed to go out. Could you imagine anyone making up the fire at a time like that? A pale gray powdery dust glowed red still in one patch at the heart of it, and as he watched, died. Later on, he had those ashes analyzed. All the time he was up there the dog howled. Someone shut it up in a distant room, but its long, drawn-out cries pursued him up the road on his way to see Joseph and Monica Peterlee.

He remembered wondering, not relevantly, if she dressed like that to sit down at table, to watch television. At nine o'clock at night she was still in her crossover overall, her black wellies. Her husband was a bigger and heavier version of his brother, three or four years older, his hair iron-gray where Tom's had been brown, his belly fat and slack where Tom's had been flat. They alibied each other, uselessly, and Joe had no alibi for the relevant time. He had been out shooting rabbits, he said, and produced his shotgun and shotgun license.

"They done Tom in for the money," he told Wexford sagely. He spoke as if, without his proffered information, such a solution would never have occurred to the police. "I told him. I said to him time and again, I said, you don't want to leave that laying about, not even for an hour, not even in daylight. What you got a safe for if you don't use it? I said that, didn't I, girl?"

His wife confirmed that he had indeed said it. Over and over. Wexford had the impression she would have confirmed anything he said. For peace, for a quiet life. It was two days later that, interviewing them again, he asked about the relationship between Tom and Heather Peterlee.

"They was a very happy couple," Joe said. "Never a cross word in all the ten years they was married."

Wexford later wondered what Dora would have said if he had made such a remark about relatives of his. Or Burden's wife Jenny if he had. Something dry, surely. There would have been some quick intervention, some "Oh, come on, how would you know?" or "You weren't a fly on the wall." But Monica said nothing. She smiled nervously. Her husband looked at her and she stopped smiling.

❑   ❑   ❑

The ram raiders were expected to have another go the following Saturday night. Instead they came on Friday, late shopping night at Stowerton Brook Buyers' Heaven, less than an hour after the shops closed. Another stolen Land Rover burst through the entrance doors, followed by a stolen Range Rover and a BMW. This time the haul was from Electronic World but similar to that taken the previous time.

The men in those three vehicles got away with an astonishing thirty-five thousand pounds' worth of equipment.

This time Burden had not been nearby on his way home. No one had, since the Stowerton Brook industrial site where Buyers' Heaven was lay totally deserted by night, emptier by far than Kingsmarkham town center. The two guard dogs that kept watch over the neighboring builders' supplies yard had been destroyed a month before in the purge on dangerous breeds.

Burden had been five miles away, talking to Carol Fox and her husband Raymond. To Burden, who never much noticed any woman's appearance but his wife's, she was simply rather above average good-looking. In her mid-thirties, ten years younger than Heather, she was brightly dressed and vivacious. It was Wexford who described her as one of that group or category that seems to have more natural color than most women, with her pure red hair, glowing luminous skin, ivory and pink, and her eyes of gentian blue. He said nothing about the unnatural color that decorated Mrs. Fox's lips, nails, and eyelids to excess. Burden assessed her as "just a cockney with an awful voice." Privately, he thought of her as common. She was loud and coarse, a strange friend for the quiet, reserved, and mousy Heather.

The husband she had returned to after a six-month separation was thin and toothy with hagridden eyes, some sort of salesman. He seemed proud of her and exaggeratedly pleased to have her back. On that particular evening, the case not much more than a week old, he was anxious to assure Burden and anyone else who would listen that his and his wife's parting had been no more than a "trial," an experimental living-apart to refresh their relationship. They were together again now for good. Their separation hadn't been a success but a source of misery to both of them.

Carol said nothing. Asked by Burden to go over with him once more the events of October 10, she reaffirmed six-twenty as the time she and Heather had gone out. Yes, there had been a basket of logs just inside the back door. She hadn't seen any money on the counter or the dresser. Tom had been drying dishes when she came in. He was alive and well when they left, putting the dishes away in the cupboard.

"I should be so lucky," said Carol Fox with a not very affectionate glance at her husband.

"Did you like Tom Peterlee, Mrs. Fox?"

Was it his imagination or had Raymond Fox's expression changed minutely? It would be too much to say that he had winced. Burden repeated his question.

"He was always pleasant," she said. "I never saw much of him."

The results came from the lab disclosing that a piece of animal bone had been among the stove ashes. Burden had found out, that first evening, what the Peterlees had had for their evening meal: lamb chops with potatoes and cabbage Tom had grown himself. The remains were put into the bin for the compost heap, never into the stove. Bones, cooked or otherwise—the Peterlees weren't particular—were put on the back doorstep for the dog.

What had become of the missing money? It wasn't a large enough sum for the spending of it by any particular individual to be noticeable. They searched the house a sec-

ond time, observing the empty safe, the absence of any jewelry, even of a modest kind, in Heather's possession, the absence of books, any kind of reading matter, or any sign of
the generally accepted contributions to gracious living.

Heather Peterlee shut herself up in the house, and when
approached said nothing. Questioned, she stared dumbly
and remained dumb. Everyone explained her silence as due
to her grief. Wexford, without much hope of anything coming of it, asked to remove the film from the camera that had
weighted down the missing notes. She shrugged, muttered
that he could have it, he was welcome, and turned her face
to the wall. But when he came to look, he found no film in
the camera.

Burden said Wexford's continued visits to Arlene Heddon were an obsession, the Chief Constable that they were a
waste of time. Since his second visit she had given precisely
the same answers to all the questions he asked—the same,
that is, as on that second occasion. He wondered how she did
it. Either it was the transparent truth or she had total recall.
In that case, why did it differ from what she had said the first
time he questioned her? Now all was perfect consistency.

If she made a personal comment there might be something new, but she rarely did. Every time he referred to Tom
Peterlee as her stepfather she corrected him by saying, "I
called him Tom," and if he spoke of Joseph and Monica as
her uncle and aunt she told him they weren't her uncle and
aunt. Carol Fox was her mother's great friend, she had
known her for years, but she, Arlene, knew Carol scarcely
at all.

"I never heard of Carol walking the dog with my mother,
but I wouldn't. I wasn't interested in Carol."

Sometimes Gary Wyatt was there. When Wexford came

he always left. He always had a muttered excuse about having to see someone about something and being late already. One Monday—it was usually Mondays and Thursdays that Wexford went to the caravan—he asked Gary to wait a moment. Had he thought any more about giving details of where he was between six forty-five and seven-thirty that evening? Gary hadn't. He had been in the pub, the Red Rose at Edenwick.

"No one remembers seeing you."

"That's their problem."

"It may become yours, Gary. You didn't like Tom Peterlee, did you? Isn't it a fact that Tom refused to let you and Arlene have the caravan Mrs. Fox lived in because you'd left your wife and children?"

"That was the pot calling the kettle," said Gary.

"And what does that mean?"

Nothing, they said. It meant nothing. He hadn't been referring to Tom. A small smile crossed Arlene's face and was gone. Gary went out to see someone about something, an appointment for which he was already late, and Wexford began asking about Heather's behavior when she came home after her walk.

"She didn't throw herself at him," Arlene said glibly without, it seemed, a vestige of feeling. "She knelt down and sort of held his head and cuddled it. She got his blood on her. Carol and me, we made her get up and then she started banging her face on that counter."

It was the same as last time, always the same.

❑   ❑   ❑

There had been no appeals to the public for witnesses to come forward. Witnesses to what? Heather Peterlee's alibi was supplied by Carol Fox, and Wexford couldn't see why she should have lied or the two of them been in cahoots. Friend she might be, but not such a friend as to perjure herself to save a woman who had motivelessly murdered an ideal husband.

He wondered about the bone fragment. But they had a dog. It was hardly too far-fetched to imagine a dog's bone getting in among the logs for the stove. Awkward, yes, but awkward, inexplicable things do happen. It was still hard for him to accept that Arlene had simply taken it for granted her mother was out walking the dog with Carol Fox when she scarcely seemed to know that Carol lived there. And he had never really been able to swallow that business about Heather banging her face against the counter. Carol had only said, "Oh, yes, she did," and Heather herself put her hands over her mouth and turned her face to the wall.

Then a curious thing happened that began to change everything.

An elderly man who had been a regular customer at the farm shop asked to speak to Wexford. He was a widower who shopped and cooked for himself, living on the state pension and a pension from the Mid-Sussex Water Authority.

Frank Waterton began by apologizing, he was sure it was nothing, he shouldn't really be troubling Wexford, but this was a matter that had haunted him. He had always meant to do something about it, though he was never sure what. That was why he had, in the event, done nothing.

"What is it, Mr. Waterton? Why not tell me and I'll decide if it's nothing." The old man looked at him almost wistfully. "No one will blame you if it's nothing. You'll still have been public-spirited and have done your duty."

Wexford didn't even know then that it was connected with the Peterlee case. Because he was due to pay one of his twice-weekly calls on Arlene Heddon, he was impatient and did his best not to let his impatience show.

"It's to do with what I noticed once or twice when I went shopping for my bits and pieces at Feverel's," he said, and then Wexford ceased to feel exasperated or to worry about getting to Arlene on time. "It must have been back in June the first time. I know it was June on account of the strawberries were in. I can see her now looking through the strawberries to get me a nice punnet and when she lifted her face up—well, I was shocked. I was really shocked. She was bruised like someone had been knocking her about. She'd a black eye and a cut on her cheek. I said, You've been in the wars, Mrs. Peterlee, and she said she'd had a fall and hit herself on the sink."

"You say that was the first time?"

"That's right. I sort of half-believed her when she said that, but not the next time. Not when I went in there again when the Coxes apples first came in—must have been late September—and her face was black and blue all over again. And she'd got her wrist strapped up—well, bandaged. I didn't comment, not that time. I reckoned it wouldn't be— well, tactful.

"I just thought I ought to come and tell someone. It's been preying on my mind ever since I heard about Tom Peterlee getting done in. I sort of hesitated and hemmed and hawed. If it had been *her* found killed I'd have been in like a shot, I can tell you."

He made it to Arlene's only a quarter of an hour late.

Because it fascinated him, hearing her give all those same answers, parrotlike, except that the voice this parrot mimicked was her own, he asked her all the same things over again. The question about her mother's bruised face he left till last, to have the effect of a bombshell.

First of all, he got the same stuff. "She knelt down and took hold of his head and sort of cuddled it. That's how she got his blood on her. Me and Carol pulled her off him and lifted her up and she started banging her face on the counter."

"Was she banging her face on the counter in June, Miss Heddon? Was she doing the same thing in September? And how about her bandaged wrist?"

Arlene Heddon didn't know. She looked him straight in the eye, both her eyes into both his, and said she didn't know.

"I never saw her wrist bandaged."

He turned deliberately from her hypnotic gaze and looked around the caravan. They had acquired a microwave since he was last there. An electric jug kettle had replaced the old chrome one. Presents from Grandma? The old witch was reputed to be well-off. It was said that none of the money she had made from selling off acres of her land in building lots had found its way into her sons' pockets. He had noticed a new car parked outside the railway carriage cottage and wouldn't have been surprised to learn that she replaced hers every couple of years.

"It'll be Tuesday next week, not Monday, Miss Heddon," he said as he left.

"Suit yourself."

"Gary found himself a job yet?"

"What job? You must be joking."

"Perhaps I am. Perhaps there's something hilarious in the idea of either of you working. I mean, have you ever given it a thought? Earning your living is what I'm talking about."

She shut the door hard between them.

After that, inquiries among the people who had known them elicited plenty of descriptions of Mrs. Peterlee's visible injuries. Regular customers at the farm shop remembered her bandaged arm. One spoke of a black eye so bad that it had closed up and on the following day Heather Peterlee had covered it with a shade. She explained a scab on her upper lip as a cold sore, but the customer to whom she had told this story hadn't believed her.

The myth of the ideal husband was beginning to fade. Only the Peterlees themselves continued to support it, and Monica Peterlee, when Burden asked her about it, seemed stricken dumb with fear. It was as if he had put his finger on the sorest part of a trauma and reawakened everything that caused the wound.

"I don't want to talk about it. You can't make me. I don't want to know."

Joseph treated the suggestion as a monstrous calumny on his dead brother. He blustered. "You want to be very careful what you're insinuating. Tom's dead and he can't defend himself, so you lot think you can say anything. The police aren't gods anymore, you want to remember that. There's not an evening goes by when you don't see it on the telly, another lot of coppers up in court for making things up they'd writ down and saying things what never happened."

His wife was looking at him the way a mouse in a corner looks at a cat that has temporarily mislaid it. Burden wasn't

26

going to question Heather. They left her severely alone as they began to build up a case against her.

"What would you do if your husband knocked you about?" Wexford asked his wife.

"Are we talking about you or just any old husband?"

He grinned. "Not me. One of those you didn't marry but might have."

"Well, I know it's the conventional thing to say one wouldn't put up with it. You know, 'He wouldn't do it a second time,' that kind of thing, but that may be a bit shallow. If he was filled with remorse afterwards, for instance, or seemed to be. If one had no other means of support and nowhere else to go. If there were children. And, well, if it doesn't sound too silly, if one loved him."

"Could you? Go on loving him?"

"Heaven knows. I won't say women are strange. *People* are strange."

"You said, 'He wouldn't do it a second time.' I wonder if there comes the final straw to break her back and he doesn't do it a *twenty*-second time."

Jenny Burden said only that she wouldn't get herself into that position. She'd know before she married him.

"One way she might know," Wexford said when this was passed on to him, "was from what she heard of her future father-in-law's behavior. There's a lot in what the psychologists say about the chain of family brutality. The child who is abused abuses his own children. Is it also true that the sons who see their mother battered by their father batter their own wives? They accept this behavior as the marital norm?"

"Didn't you tell me old Mrs. Peterlee said her husband knocked her about until she took a knife to him?"

Wexford nodded. "That was her last straw and she retaliated. She danced on his grave, Mike. I wonder if Heather has it in mind to dance on Tom's?''

The day after the third ram raid—this time on the Kingsbrook Centre itself in the middle of Kingsmarkham—Wexford was back in Arlene Heddon's caravan and Arlene was saying, ''I never saw her wrist bandaged.''

''Miss Heddon, you know your stepfather repeatedly assaulted your mother. He knocked her about, gave her black eyes, cut her cheek. His brother Joseph doubtless hands out the same treatment to his wife. What have you got to gain by pretending you knew nothing about it?''

''She knelt on the floor and lifted up his head and sort of cuddled it. That's how she got blood on her. Me and Carol sort of pulled her off him and then she started banging—''

Wexford stopped her. ''No. She got those bruises because Tom hit her in the face. I don't know why. Do you know why? Maybe it was over money, the shop takings he left on the dresser. Or maybe she'd protested about his asking for more rent from her friend Carol Fox. If your mother argued with him he reacted by hitting her. That was his way.''

''If you say so.''

''No, Miss Heddon. It's not what I say, it's what you say.''

He waited for her to rejoin with ''I never saw her wrist bandaged,'' but she lifted her eyes and he could have sworn there was amusement in them, a flash of it that came and went. She astounded him by what she said. It was the last thing he expected. She fidgeted for a moment or two with the channel changer on the divider between them, lifted her eyes, and said slowly, ''Carol Fox was Tom's girlfriend.''

He digested this, saw fleetingly a host of possible implications, said, ''What, precisely, do you mean by that term?''

28

She was almost contemptuous. "What everyone means. His girlfriend. His lover. What me and Gary are."

□   □   □

"Not much point in denying it, is there?" said Carol Fox.

"I'm surprised you didn't give us this piece of information, Mr. Fox," Wexford said.

When her husband said nothing, Carol broke in impatiently. "Oh, he's ashamed. Thinks it's a reflection on his manhood or whatever. I told him, you can't keep a thing like that dark, so why bother?"

"You kept it dark from us deliberately for a month."

She shrugged, unrepentant. "I felt a bit bad about Heather, to be honest with you. It was like Tom said I could live in this caravan on his land. He never said it was right next door. Still, there was another girl he'd had four or five years back he actually brought to live in the house. He called her the au pair, as if those Peterlees weren't one generation from gypsies when all's said and done."

"Then I take it his visit to you that evening had nothing to do with raising the rent?"

The husband got up and left the room. Wexford didn't try to stop him. His presence hadn't much inhibited his wife, but his absence freed her further. She smiled just a little. "It's not what you're thinking. We had a drink."

"A bit odd, wasn't it, you going out for a walk with his wife? Or didn't she know? That's pretty hard to believe, Mrs. Fox."

"Of course she knew. She hated me. And I can't say I was too keen on her. That wasn't true about us often going out

29

together. That walk, that night, I fixed it up because I wanted to talk to her. I wanted to tell her I was leaving, it was all over between me and Tom, and I was going back to Ray." She drew in a long breath. "I'll be honest with you, it was a physical thing. The way he looked—well, between you and me, I couldn't get enough of it. Maybe it's all worked out for the best. But the fact is, it'd have been different if Tom'd have said he'd leave her, but he wouldn't and I'd had it."

Wexford said, when he and Burden were out in the car, "I was beginning to see Heather's alibi going down the drain. Her best friend lying for her. Not now. I can't see Tom's girlfriend alibiing the wife she wanted out of the way."

"Well, no. Especially not alibiing the woman who'd killed the man she loved or once had loved. It looks as if we start again."

"Does anyone but Heather have a motive? What was in it for Arlene or Gary Wyatt? The man's own mother's capable of anything her strength allows her, but I don't think her strength would have allowed her this. Joseph had nothing to gain by Tom's death—the farm becomes Heather's—and it's evident all Monica wants is a quiet life. So we're left with the marauder who goes about the countryside murdering smallholders for three hundred and sixty quid."

Next morning an envelope arrived addressed to him. It contained nothing but a photographic film processor's chit, which was also a receipt for one pound. The receipt was on paper headed with the name of a pharmacist in the York Crest Centre. Wexford guessed the origin of the film before he had Sergeant Martin collect the processed shots. Arlene, at home to him on Tuesday, was back at her parrot game.

"I haven't lived at home since I was seventeen. I don't know all the friends my mother's got. I didn't know whether Carol took the dog out or what. Tom sometimes took him out, and my mother did. I never heard of Carol going with my mother, but I wouldn't. I wasn't interested in Carol."

"This is reaching the proportions of a psychosis, Miss Heddon."

She knew what he meant. He didn't have to explain. He could see comprehension in her eyes and her small satisfied smile. Others would have asked when all this was going to stop, when would he leave it alone. Not she. She would give all the same answers to his questions infinitely, and every few weeks throw in a bombshell, as she had when she told him of Carol Fox's place in the Peterlees' lives. Always supposing, of course, that she had more bombshells to throw.

He knocked on the old witch's door. After rather a long time she came. Wexford wasn't invited in and he could see she already had company. An elderly man with a white beard, but wearing jeans and red leather cowboy boots, was standing by the fireplace pouring wine from a half-empty bottle into two glasses.

She gave him the grin that cracked her face into a thousand wrinkles and showed her remarkable teeth.

"I had half an hour going spare, Mrs. Peterlee, so I thought I'd use it asking you where you were between six and seven-thirty on the evening your son was killed."

She put her head to one side. "I reckoned I'd keep you all guessing."

"And now you're going to tell me," he said patiently.

"Why not?" She turned and shouted over her shoulder at a pitch absurdly loud for the distance, "If that one's finished, Eric, you can go and open another. It's on the kitchen table." Wexford was favored with a wink. "I was with my boyfriend. *Him.* At his place. I always drop in for a quick one before the meeting." She very nearly made him blush. "A quick *drink,*" she said. "You can ask him when he comes back. Rude bunch of buggers you cops are. It's written all over your face what you're thinking. Well, he'd marry me tomorrow if I said the word, but I'm shy, I've been bitten once. He may be nice as pie now and all lovey-dovey, but it's another story when they've got the ring on your finger. Don't want another one knocking me to kingdom come when his tea's five minutes late on the table."

"Is that why Tom beat up Heather, because his meal was late?"

If she was taken aback she didn't show it. "Come on, they don't need a reason, not when the drink's in them. It's just you being there and not as strong as them and scared too, that's enough for them. You needn't look like that. I don't suppose you do like the sound of it. You want to've been on the receiving end. Okay, Eric, I'm coming."

Now that he no longer suspected her, after he had left her alone for a month, he went to Feverel's and saw Heather Peterlee. It was the night of the third ram raid, and they knew it was coming when a Volvo Estate and a Land Rover were reported stolen during the day. But that was still three or four hours off.

Abused women have a look in common. Wexford castigated himself for not having seen it when he first came to the house. It had nothing to do with bruises and not much to do with a cowed, beaten way of holding themselves. That washed-out tired drained appearance told it all, if you knew what you were looking for.

She was very thin, but not with the young vigorous slimness of her daughter or the wiriness of her mother-in-law. Her leanness showed slack muscles in her arms and stringy tendons at her wrists. There were hollows under her cheekbones and her mouth was already sunken. The benefit of weeks without Tom had not yet begun to show. Heather Peterlee had neglected herself and her home, had perhaps spent her time of widowhood in silent brooding here in this ugly dark house with only the spaniel for company.

The dog barked and snarled when Wexford came. To silence it she struck it too brutally across the muzzle. Violence begets violence, he thought. You receive it and store it up and then you transmit it—on to whoever or whatever is feebler than you.

But even now she denied it. Sitting opposite him in a drab cotton dress with a thick knitted cardigan dragged shawl-like around her, she repudiated any suggestion that Tom had been less than good and gentle. As for Carol, yes it was true Tom had offered her the caravan and not she. Tom had been told by a friend she wanted a place to live. What friend? She didn't know the name. And the "au pair"?

"You've been talking to my daughter."

Wexford admitted that this was indeed the case, though not to what weary extent it was true.

"Arlene imagines things. She's got too much imagination." A spark of vitality made a small change in her when she spoke of her daughter. Her voice became a fraction more animated. "She's brainy, is Arlene, she's a bright one. Wanted to go in for the police, you know."

"I'm sorry?"

"Get to be a policewoman or whatever they call them now."

"A police officer," said Wexford. "Did she really? What stopped that, then?"

"Took up with that Gary, didn't she?"

It was hardly an answer, but Wexford didn't pursue it. He didn't ask about her husband's involvement with Carol Fox, either. He had proof of that, not only in Carol's own admission but in the film from Tom Peterlee's camera. All the shots were of Carol, three nudes taken with a flash inside Feverel's caravan. They were decorous enough, not the kind of thing to raise a protest from any pharmacist Tom might have taken them to, for Carol had been coy in her posing, even skilled in turning her body and smiling over her shoulder.

He studied the three photographs again that evening. Their setting, not their voluptuous subject, made them pathetic. Sordidness of background, a window with a sagging net curtain, a coat hanging up, a glimpse of an encrusted pot on a hot plate, gave an air of attempts at creating pornography in some makeshift studio. Erotica, for Wexford, required a total absence of ugliness, and Carol Fox had succeeded in that not uncommon achievement of sexiness without beauty.

Not that a hope of titillation was his motive for looking at the pictures. He looked rather coldly and even sadly. The identity of the sender of the processor's chit wasn't a problem. He had known that, if not from the moment he took it from its envelope, at least long before forensics matched with an existing set the fingerprints on the paper. He knew who had handed over the counter the film and the pound deposit. It was not even the subject of the shots that predominantly concerned him now. His slight depression vanished and he was suddenly alert. From those pictures he suddenly knew who had killed Tom Peterlee and why.

❑   ❑   ❑

The police were waiting, virtually encircling the Kingsbrook Centre, when the ram raiders arrived. This time there were only four of them, all inside the stolen Land Rover. If others were following through the narrow streets of the town center, some prior warning turned them back. The same warning perhaps, maybe no more than feeling or intuition, that halted the Land Rover on the big paved forecourt from which the center's entrance doors opened.

At first the watchers thought only that the Land Rover was reversing, prior to performing its backward ramming of the doors. It was a few seconds before it became clear that this was a three-point turn, forward up to the fifteen-foot-high brick wall, reverse toward the doors, then, while they braced themselves for the crash of the doors going down and the Land Rover backing through, it shot forward again and was away through the alley into High Street.

But it never entered the wider road. Its occupants left it to block the exit, flung all four doors open, leapt out, and dispersed. The police, there in thirty seconds, found an empty vehicle, with no trace of any occupancy but its owner's and not a print to be found.

❑   ❑   ❑

He said to Burden before they made the arrest, "You see, she told us she didn't possess a raincoat and we didn't find one, but in this photo a raincoat is hanging up inside the caravan."

Burden took the magnifying glass from him and looked. "Bright emerald green and the buttons that sort of bone that is part white, part brown."

"She came into the kitchen when she said she did, or maybe five minutes earlier. I think it was true she'd finished with Tom, but that she meant to go for a long walk with Heather in order to tell her so, that was a fiction. She wore the raincoat because it was already drizzling and maybe because she knew she looked nice in it. She came to tell Heather she'd be leaving and no doubt that Heather could have him and welcome.

"Did she know Tom beat his wife? Maybe and maybe not. No doubt, she thought that if Tom and she had ever got together permanently he wouldn't beat *her*. But that's by the way. She came into the kitchen and saw Heather crouched against the counter and Tom hitting her in the face.

"It's said that a woman can't really defend herself against a brutal man, but another woman can defend her. What happened to Carol Fox, Mike? Pure anger? Total disillusionment with Tom Peterlee? Some pull of the great sisterhood of women? Perhaps we shall find out. She snatched up a log out of that basket, a strong oak log, and struck him over the back of the head with it. And again and again. Once she'd started she went on in a frenzy—until he was dead."

"One of them," said Burden, "and I'd say Carol, wouldn't you?—acted with great presence of mind then, organizing what they must do. Carol took off the raincoat that was covered with blood and thrust it along with the weapon into the stove. In the hour or so before we got there everything was consumed but part of one of the buttons.''

"Carol washed her hands, put on one of Heather's jackets. They took the dog and went out down to the river. It was never, as we thought, Carol providing an alibi for Heather. It was Heather alibiing Carol. They would stay out for three quarters of an hour, come back and 'find' the body, or even try to get rid of the body, clean up the kitchen, pretend that Tom had gone away. What they didn't foresee was Arlene's arrival."

"But Arlene came an hour early," Burden said.

"Arlene assumed that her mother had done it and she would think she knew why. The mouse in the corner attacked when the cat's attention was diverted. The worm turned as Grandma turned when her husband struck her once too often."

He said as much to Arlene Heddon next day after Carol Fox had been charged with murder. "You only told me she was Tom's girlfriend when you thought things were looking bad for your mother. You reasoned that if a man's mistress gave a man's wife an alibi it was bound to seem genuine. In case I didn't believe you and she denied it, you sent me the receipt they gave you when you took the film you'd removed from Tom Peterlee's camera along to the York Crest Centre to be processed. I suppose your mother told you the kind of pictures he took."

She shrugged, said rather spitefully, "You weren't so clever. All that about me knowing who'd killed Tom. I didn't know, I thought it was my mother."

He glanced around the caravan, took in the radio and

tape player, microwave oven, video, and his eye fell on the small black rectangle he had in the past, without a closer look, taken for a remote-control channel changer. Now he thought how lazy you would have to be, how incapacitated almost, to need to change channels by this means. Almost anywhere in here you were within an arm's length of the television set. He picked it up.

It was a tape recorder, five inches long, two inches wide, flat, black. The end with the red "on" light was and always had been turned toward the kitchen area.

So confident had she been in her control of things and perhaps in her superior intelligence that she had not even stripped the tiny label off its underside. Nixon's, York Crest, £54.99—he was certain Arlene hadn't paid fifty-five pounds for it.

"You can't have that!" She was no longer cool.

"I'll give you a receipt for it," he said, and then, "Gary, no doubt, was with his pals that evening planning the first ram raid. I don't know where, but I know it wasn't the Red Rose at Edenwick."

She was quite silent, staring at him. He fancied she would have liked to snatch the recorder from him but did not quite dare. Serendipity or a long experience in reading faces and drawing conclusions made him say, "Let's hear what you've been taping on here, Miss Heddon."

He heard his own voice, then hers. As clear as a phone conversation. It was a good tape recorder. He thought, Yes, Gary Wyatt was involved in the first ram raid, the one that took place after the murder and after the first time I came here to talk to her. From then on, from the second time . . .

"I didn't know Carol very well."

"But she was a close friend of your mother's . . ." His voice tailed away into cracklings.

"I haven't lived at home since I was seventeen. I don't know all the friends my mother's got . . ."

"So that was how you did it," he said. "You recorded our conversations and learned your replies off by heart. That was a way to guarantee your answers would never vary."

In a stiff wooden voice she said, "If you say so."

He got up. "I don't think Gary's going to be with you much longer, Miss Heddon. You'll be visiting him once a month, if you're so inclined. Some say there's a very thin line dividing the cop from the criminal, they've the same kind of intelligence. Your mother tells me you once had ambitions to be a police officer. You've got off to a bad start, but maybe it's not too late."

With the recorder in his pocket, stooping as he made his way out of the caravan, he turned back and said, "If you like the idea, give me a ring."

He closed the door behind him and descended the steps onto the muddy field and the cinder path.

LIZZIE'S LOVER

"The rain set early in tonight," she said.

She came into the house and he shut the door behind her. Her head had been uncovered and her long fair hair was wet. He smiled at her. "D'you know what you said?"

"I'm sorry?"

"The rain set early in tonight. That's the first line of 'Porphyria's Lover.' " He looked into her face for comprehension, saw none. "Browning. It's a poem, Lizzie. Did you never do it at school?"

He took her coat, which was very wet, and, having thought better of his first idea, the hooks on the hall wall, draped it over the back of a chair. The house was small and low-ceilinged, a little brick house in a terrace in the far reaches of a South London suburb, unheard of, far away from underground stations and bus stops.

"Did you say Porphyria?" she said.

"That's right."

"Porphyria's a disease, Michael. I don't know why it's called that, but it is. Your urine goes purple."

"Browning called the girl in his poem Porphyria before they named the disease. There's a sort of marble, too, called porphyry. It means purple. *Porphyra*, Greek, purple."

"The things you know," she said. "You've got a hair dryer, haven't you? I'd like to dry my hair."

Michael couldn't bear the noise. "The dryer broke and I threw it out," he lied. "I've lit a fire. We'll have some wine and you can dry your hair by the fire."

She was wearing a long skirt of a bluish-mauve color with a dark purple top of velvet and a fine violet chiffon scarf. The hem of the skirt was wet. He thought how absurd it was that women who had emancipated themselves into trousers should revert back to what their great-grandmothers wore—and from choice. The fire was half dead, a smoldering flameless mass. While he opened the wine, she knelt down and worked at the fire with the fancy brass bellows he had bought in a junk shop.

He recited softly, " 'She shut the cold out and the storm, And kneeled and made the cheerless grate Blaze up, and all the cottage warm.' "

"Hardly that," she said, and she laughed. "Is that more of 'Porphyria'?"

"I was doing it with the kids in class today, and now you seem to be acting it out. Here's your wine. She'd come to his house out of the rain, she had wet hair too, yellow hair, Browning says, which yours is, I suppose."

"Yellow? I don't like the sound of that. What's your poem about? I know you're dying to tell me."

He watched her dip her head down and spread out the hair in a wide golden fan. The firelight made the separate strands sparkle.

"I don't know the whole thing by heart," he said, "only bits. There's a feast in it, which reminds me I should start getting us some food. Or do you want to go out to eat?"

"I'm not hungry." She began passing a comb through

her hair. It made an electric crackling. "Don't let's eat yet."

"All right, then," he said. "Come and sit here beside me."

The little room had a sofa in it, covered with a piece of red and purple tapestry. Two table lamps had dark red shades, and these he left on while turning out the central light. The room became cozy and at the same time seemed smaller. Michael sat on the sofa and patted the cushion next to him. When she was sitting beside him he lifted one of her hands and laid his in it.

" 'She put my arm about her waist,' " he said. "That's right, put my arm round your waist. 'And made her smooth white shoulder bare.' " Gently he drew the purple velvet neckline down, exposing her upper arm. "Yours is more tanned than white. Victorian girls avoided the sun."

"A lot of people would say that was wise. Go on with the poem."

"I told you I can't remember it all. She makes him rest his cheek on her bare shoulder and then she spreads her hair 'o'er all,' meaning his face, one supposes."

"Like this?"

Lizzie laid her hair across his face and her shoulder like a veil. He shook himself and sat up because he disliked getting hairs in his mouth. "More wine?"

"Yes, please."

He refilled her glass and brought it back to her. When she made a move to pick it up he took hold of her hand, held it, and bringing his mouth to hers, kissed her lingeringly. He smoothed the long hair away from her face, undid the knot in the purple scarf, and kissed the hollow in her throat.

"Is that what the lover did with Porphyria?" she asked him softly.

43

"No, I don't believe he did. He didn't kiss her—not then. He was pleased because she'd come through wind and rain, and not so pleased because she wouldn't give herself to him forever."

"If that means sleep with him, Victorians didn't, did they?"

"I expect some did," said Michael. "Anyway, he says that 'passion sometimes would prevail,' and in fact it was passion which had driven her to him that night."

"Must have been the same thing with me," said Lizzie. "It took me nearly two hours to get here, what with the Victoria Line down and the buses all coming at once and then none for half an hour. Only passion kept me going."

" 'Be sure I looked up at her eyes,' " said Michael, " 'Happy and proud; at last I knew Porphyria worshipped me.' "

"Was she married? Like me?"

"Browning doesn't say. But he described her as 'perfectly pure and good,' so one would suppose not. Unfaithful wives were criminals in his day."

Lizzie looked away and drank some of her wine. Then she held Michael's wrist and lightly stroked the palm of his hand. She said dreamily, "What happened next?"

"He strangled her."

She dropped his hand as if it burned her and retreated into the corner of the sofa. *"What?"*

"He strangled her with her own hair. To keep her for himself. Forever. 'I found,' he says, 'A thing to do, and all her hair In one long yellow string I wound Three times her little throat around . . .' "

"And you do this poem with the kids at school?"

"They're sixteen, Lizzie. They're not babies."

She edged back nearer to him. "It wouldn't work. You couldn't strangle someone with her own hair."

"Why not, if it was long enough?"

For answer she took hold of her own hair in one thick hank, golden and smooth, and held it out to him on her hand like someone offering an object for sale. He took the hair in both hands and twisted it once, drew it down past her right ear and across her throat. At first he wound it loosely, then, pulling it tighter, succeeded in making almost two circuits of her smooth brown neck.

" 'Her cheek once more,' " he said, " 'Blushed bright beneath my burning kiss.' "

"He kissed her on the *cheek?*" said Lizzie.

"With the Victorian I sometimes think that was a euphemism for mouth." Michael brought his to hers, but as he touched her skin deflected his lips to where the corner of mouth and cheek met. As he pressed his lips on the warm soft skin he took a firmer hold of her hair and gave a sharp tug.

"Michael!" It was almost a scream.

He was pulling on the skein of hair as hard as he could. Suddenly he released her. She pulled down her hair with both hands. "For God's sake!"

"You were right. It can't be done. Your hair's not long enough."

"Just as well. You frightened me for a moment."

"Did I?" he said. "Surely not."

With both hands he smoothed her hair back over her shoulders. He put his hand under her chin and lifted it. Her eyes were doubtful. He looked deep into them.

"It was a way of keeping her forever, wasn't it? No going back to the husband when the evening was over, no more pride or 'vainer ties' to dissever. I can understand that.''

His hands were on her shoulders now and the eyes were mesmerizing. Hers glazed over and her mouth trembled. He took hold of the two ends of the purple chiffon scarf, crossed them, and in a hard swift movement, pulled them tight. She screamed, but no sound came. Porphyria hadn't fought at all, but Lizzie fought, thrashing and kicking and flailing with her hands, choking and gasping. But when the struggles were over she, too, lay still, her head fallen into his lap.

He stroked the hair that hadn't been quite long enough. He quoted softly, " 'And thus we sit together now, And all night long we have not stirred, And yet God has not said a word!' ''

BURNING END

After she had been doing it for a year, it occurred to Linda that looking after Betty fell to her lot because she was a woman. Betty was Brian's mother, not hers, and Betty had two other children, both sons, both unmarried men. No one had ever suggested that either of them should take a hand in looking after their mother. Betty had never much liked Linda, had sometimes hinted that Brian had married beneath him, and once, in the heat of temper, said that Linda was "not good enough" for her son, but still it was Linda who cared for her now. Linda felt a fool for not having thought of it in these terms before.

She knew she would not get very far talking about it to Brian. Brian would say—and did say—that this was women's work. A man couldn't perform intimate tasks for an old woman; it wasn't fitting. When Linda asked why not, he told her not to be silly, everyone knew why not.

"Suppose it had been your dad that was left, suppose he'd been bedridden, would I have looked after him?"

Brian looked over the top of his evening paper. He was holding the remote in his hand, but he didn't turn down the sound. "He wasn't left, was he?"

"No, but if he had been?"

"I reckon you would have. There isn't anyone else, is there? It's not as if the boys were married."

Every morning after Brian had gone out into the farm-yard and before she left for work, Linda drove down the road, turned left at the church into the lane, and after a mile came to the very small cottage on the very large piece of land where Betty had lived since the death of her husband twelve years before. Betty slept downstairs in the room at the back. She was always awake when Linda got there, although that was invariably before seven-thirty, and she always said she had been awake since five.

Linda got her up and changed the incontinence pad. Most mornings she had to change the sheets as well. She washed Betty, put her into a clean nightgown and clean bedjacket, socks and slippers, and while Betty shouted and moaned, lifted and shoved her as best she could into the armchair she would remain in all day. Then it was breakfast. Sweet milky tea and bread and butter and jam. Betty wouldn't use the feeding cup with the spout. What did Linda think she was, a baby? She drank from a cup, and un-less Linda had remembered to cover her up with the muslin squares that had indeed once had their use for babies, the tea would go all down the clean nightgown and Betty would have to be changed again.

After Linda had left her and gone off to work the district nurse would come, though not every day, not for certain. The Meals-on-Wheels lady would come and give Betty her midday dinner, bits and pieces in foil containers, all labeled with the names of their contents. At some point Brian would come. Brian would "look in." Not to *do* anything, not to clear anything away or give his mother something to eat or make her a cup of tea or run the vacuum cleaner around—Linda did that on Saturdays—but to sit in Betty's bedroom for ten minutes, smoking a cigarette and watching whatever was on television. Very occasionally, perhaps once a month, the brother who lived two miles away would come for ten minutes and watch television with Brian. The other brother, the one who lived ten miles away, never came at all except at Christmas.

Linda always knew if Brian had been there by the smell of smoke and the cigarette end stubbed out in the ashtray. But even if there had been no smell and no stub she would have known, because Betty always told her. Betty thought Brian was a saint and an angel to spare a moment away from the farm to visit his old mother. She could no longer speak distinctly but she was positively articulate on the subject of Brian, the most perfect son any woman ever had.

It was about five when Linda got back there. Usually the incontinence pad needed changing again, and often the nightdress too. Considering how ill she was and partially paralyzed, Betty ate a great deal. Linda made her scrambled egg or sardines on toast. She brought pastries with her from the cakeshop or, in the summer, strawberries and cream. She made more tea for Betty, and when the meal was over, somehow heaved Betty back into that bed.

The bedroom window was never opened. Betty wouldn't have it. The room smelled of urine and lavender, camphor and Meals-on-Wheels, so every day on her way to work Linda opened the window in the front room and left the doors open. It didn't make much difference, but she went on doing it. When she had got Betty to bed she washed up the day's teacups, emptied the ashtray and washed it, and put all the soiled linen into a plastic bag to take home. The question she asked Betty before she left had become meaningless, because Betty always said no, and she hadn't asked it once since having that conversation with Brian about whose job it was to look after his mother, but she asked it now.

"Wouldn't it be better if we moved you in with us, Mum?"

Betty's hearing was erratic. This was one of her deaf days.

"What?"

"Wouldn't you be better off coming to live with us?"

"I'm not leaving my home till they carry me out feet first. How many times do I have to tell you?"

Linda said all right and she was off now and she would see her in the morning. Looking rather pleased at the prospect, Betty said she would be dead by the morning.

"Not you," said Linda, which was what she always said, and so far she had always been right.

She went into the front room and closed the window. The room was furnished in a way that must have been old-fashioned even when Betty was young. In the center of it was a square dining table, around which stood six chairs with seats of faded green silk. There was a large elaborately carved sideboard but no armchairs, no small tables, no books, and no lamps but the central light, which, enveloped in a shade of parchment panels stitched together with leather thongs, was suspended directly over the glass vase that stood on a lace mat in the absolute center of the table.

For some reason, ever since the second stroke had incapacitated Betty two years before, all the post, all the junk mail and every freebie news-sheet that was delivered to the cottage ended up on this table. Every few months it was cleared away, but this hadn't been done for some time, and Linda noticed that only about four inches of the glass vase now showed above the sea of paper. The lace mat was not visible at all. She noticed something else as well.

It had been a warm sunny day, very warm for April. The cottage faced south and all afternoon the sunshine had poured through the window, was still pouring through the window, striking the neck of the vase so that the glass was too bright to look at. Where the sunstruck glass touched a sheet of paper a burning had begun. The burning glass was making a dark charred channel through the sheet of thin printed paper.

Linda screwed up her eyes. They had not deceived her. That was smoke she could see. And now she could smell burning paper. For a moment she stood there, fascinated, marveling at this phenomenon that she had heard of but had never believed in. A magnifying glass to make Boy Scouts' fires, she thought, and somewhere she had read of a forest burned down through a piece of broken glass left in a sunlit glade.

There was nowhere to put the piles of paper, so she found another plastic bag and filled that. Betty called out something, but it was only to know why she was still there. Linda dusted the table, replaced the lace mat and the glass vase, and with a bag of washing in one hand and a bag of wastepaper in the other, went home to do the washing and get an evening meal for Brian and herself and the children.

❏　　❏　　❏

The incident of the glass vase, the sun, and the burning paper had been so interesting that Linda meant to tell Brian and Andrew and Gemma all about it while they were eating. But they were also watching the finals of a quiz game

51

on television and hushed her when she started to speak. The opportunity went by and somehow there was no other until the next day. But by that time the sun and the glass setting the paper on fire no longer seemed so remarkable and Linda decided not to mention it.

Several times in the weeks that followed, Brian asked his mother if it wasn't time she came to live with them at the farm. He always told Linda of these attempts, as if in issuing this invitation he had been particularly magnanimous and self-denying. Perhaps this was because Betty responded very differently from when Linda asked her. Brian and his children, Betty said, shouldn't have to have a useless old woman under their roof, age and youth were not meant to live together, though nobody appreciated her son's generosity in asking her more than she did. Meanwhile Linda went on going to the cottage and looking after Betty for an hour every morning and an hour and a half every evening and cleaning the place on Saturdays and doing Betty's washing.

One afternoon while Brian was sitting with his mother smoking a cigarette and watching television, the doctor dropped in to pay his twice-yearly visit. He beamed at Betty, said how nice it was for her to have her devoted family around her, and on his way out told Brian it was best for the old folks to end their days at home whenever possible. If he said anything about the cigarette, Brian didn't mention it when he recounted this to Linda.

He must have picked up a pile of junk mail from the doormat and the new phone book from outside the door, for all this was lying on the table in the front room when Linda arrived at ten to five. The paper had accumulated during the past weeks, but when Linda went to look for a plastic bag she saw that the entire stock had been used up.

She made a mental note to buy some more, and in the meantime had to put the soiled sheets and Betty's two wet nightdresses into a pillowcase to take them home. The sun wasn't shining, it had been a dull day, and the forecast was for rain, so there was no danger from the conjunction of glass vase with the piles of paper. It could safely remain where it was.

On her way home it occurred to Linda that the simplest solution was to remove, not the paper but the vase. Yet, when she went back next day, she didn't remove the vase. It was a strange feeling she had, that if she moved the vase on to the mantelpiece, say, or the top of the sideboard, she would somehow have closed a door or missed a chance. Once she had moved it she would never be able to move it back again, for though she could easily have explained to anyone why she had moved it from the table, she would never be able to say why she had put it back. These thoughts frightened her, and she put them from her mind.

Linda bought a pack of fifty black plastic sacks. Betty said it was a wicked waste of money. When she was up and about she had been in the habit of burning all paper waste. All leftover food and cans and bottles got mixed up together and went out for the dustman. Betty had never heard of the environment. When Linda insisted, one hot day in July, on opening the bedroom windows, Betty said she was freezing, Linda was trying to kill her, and she would tell her son his wife was an evil woman. Linda took the curtains home and washed them, but she didn't open the bedroom window again; it wasn't worth it, it caused too much trouble.

But when Brian's brother Michael got engaged she did ask if Suzanne would take her turn looking after Betty once they were back from their honeymoon.

"You couldn't expect it of a young girl like her," Brian said.

"She's twenty-eight," said Linda.

"She doesn't look it." Brian switched on the television. "Did I tell you Geoff's been made redundant?"

"Then maybe he could help out with Betty if he hasn't got a job to go to."

Brian looked at her and shook his head gently. "He's feeling low enough as it is. It's a blow to a man's pride, that is, going on the dole. I couldn't ask him."

Why does he have to be asked? Linda thought. It's his mother.

The sun was already high in the sky when she got to the cottage at seven-thirty next morning, already edging around the house to penetrate the front-room window by ten. Linda put the junk mail on the table and took the letter and the postcard into the bedroom. Betty wouldn't look at them. She was wet through, and the bed was wet. Linda got her up and stripped off the wet clothes, wrapping Betty in a clean blanket because she said she was freezing. When she was washed and in her clean nightdress she wanted to talk about Michael's fiancée. It was one of her articulate days.

"Dirty little trollop," said Betty. "I remember her when she was fifteen. Go with anyone, she would. There's no knowing how many abortions she's had, messed all her insides up, I shouldn't wonder."

"She's very pretty, in my opinion," said Linda, "and a nice nature."

"Handsome is as handsome does. It's all that makeup and hair dye as has entrapped my poor boy. One thing, she won't set foot in this house while I'm alive."

Linda opened the window in the front room. It was

going to be a hot day, but breezy. The house could do with a good draft of air blowing through to freshen it. She thought, I wonder why no one ever put flowers in that vase, there's no point in a vase without flowers. The letters and envelopes and newsprint surrounded it so that it no longer looked like a vase but like a glass tube inexplicably poking out between a stack of paper and a telephone directory.

Brian didn't visit that day. He had started harvesting. When Linda came back at five Betty told her Michael had been in. She showed Linda the box of chocolates that was his gift, his way of "soft-soaping" her, Betty said. Not that a few violet creams had stopped her speaking her mind on the subject of that trollop.

The chocolates had gone soft and sticky in the heat. Linda said she would put them in the fridge, but Betty clutched the box to her chest, saying she knew Linda, she knew her sweet tooth, if she let that box out of her sight she'd never see it again. Linda washed Betty and changed her. While she was doing Betty's feet, rubbing cream around her toes and powdering them, Betty struck her on the head with the bedside clock, the only weapon she had at hand.

"You hurt me," said Betty. "You hurt me on purpose."

"No, I didn't, Mum. I think you've broken that clock."

"You hurt me on purpose because I wouldn't give you my chocolates my son brought me."

Brian said he was going to cut the field behind the cottage next day. Fifty acres of barley and he'd be done by mid-afternoon if the heat didn't kill him. He could have seen to his mother's needs, he'd be practically on the spot, but he didn't offer. Linda wouldn't have believed her ears if she'd heard him offer.

It was hotter than ever. It was even hot at seven-thirty. Linda washed Betty and changed the sheets. She gave her cereal for breakfast and a boiled egg and toast. From her bed Betty could see Brian going around the barley field on the combine, and this seemed to bring her enormous pleasure, though her enjoyment was tempered with pity.

"He knows what hard work is," Betty said, "he doesn't spare himself when there's a job to be done," as if Brian were cutting the fifty acres with a scythe instead of sitting up there in a cabin with twenty king-size and a can of Coke and the Walkman on his head playing Beatles songs from his youth.

Linda opened the window in the front room very wide. The sun would be around in a couple of hours to stream through that window. She adjusted an envelope on the top of the pile, moving the torn edge of its flap to brush against the glass vase. Then she moved it away again. She stood, looking at the table and the papers and the vase. A brisk draft of air made the thinner sheets of paper flutter a little. From the bedroom she heard Betty call out through closed windows to a man on a combine a quarter of a mile away, "Hallo, Brian, you all right then, are you? You keep at it, son, that's right, you got the weather on your side."

One finger stretched out, Linda lightly poked at the torn edge of the envelope flap. She didn't really move it at all. She turned her back quickly. She marched out of the room, out of the house, to the car.

❏   ❏   ❏

The fire must have started somewhere around four in the afternoon, the hottest part of that hot day. Brian had been in to see his mother when he had finished cutting the field at two. He had watched television with her and then she said she wanted to have a sleep. Those who know about these things said she had very likely died from suffocation without ever waking. That was why she hadn't phoned for help, though the phone was by her bed.

A builder driving down the lane, on his way to a barn conversion his firm was working on, called the fire brigade. They were volunteers whose headquarters was five miles away, and they took twenty minutes to get to the fire. By then Betty was dead and half the cottage destroyed. Nobody told Linda—there was hardly time—and when she got to Betty's at five it was all over. Brian and the firemen were standing about, poking at the wet black ashes with sticks, and Andrew and Gemma were in Brian's estate car outside the gate, eating potato chips.

The will was a surprise. Betty had lived in that cottage for twelve years without a washing machine or a freezer, and her television set was rented by Brian. The bed she slept in was her marriage bed, new in 1939, the cottage hadn't been painted since she moved there, and the kitchen had last been updated just after the war. But she left what seemed an enormous sum of money. Linda could hardly believe it. A third was for Geoff, a third for Michael, and the remaining third as well as the cottage—or what was left of it—for Brian.

The insurance company paid up. It was impossible to discover the cause of the fire. Something to do with the great heat, no doubt, and the thatched roof and the ancient electrical wiring that hadn't been renewed in sixty or seventy years. Linda, of course, knew better but she said nothing. She kept what she knew and let it fester inside her, giving her sleepless nights and taking away her appetite.

Brian cried noisily at the funeral. All the brothers showed excessive grief and no one told Brian to pull himself together or be a man, but put their arms around his shoulders and told him what a marvelous son he'd been and how he'd nothing to reproach himself with. Linda didn't cry, but soon after went into a black depression from which nothing could rouse her, not the doctor's tranquilizers, nor Brian's promise of a slap-up holiday somewhere, even abroad if she liked, nor people telling her Betty hadn't felt any pain but had just slipped away in her smoky sleep.

An application to build a new house on the sight of the cottage was favorably received by the planning authority and permission was granted. Why shouldn't they live in it, Brian said, he and Linda and the children? The farmhouse was ancient and awkward, difficult to keep clean, just the sort of place Londoners would like for a second home. How about moving, he said, how about a modern house, with everything you want, two bathrooms, say, and a laundry room and a sun lounge? Design it yourself and don't worry about the cost, he said, for he was concerned for his wife, who had always been so practical and efficient as well as easygoing and tractable but was now a miserable silent woman.

Linda refused to move. She didn't want a new house, especially a new house on the site of that cottage. She didn't want a holiday or money to buy clothes. She refused to touch Betty's money. Depression had forced her to give up her job, but although she was at home all day and there was no old woman to look after every morning and every evening, she did nothing in the house and Brian was obliged to get a woman in to clean. Brian could build his house and sell it, if that was what he wanted, but she wouldn't touch the money and no one could make her.

"She must have been a lot fonder of Mum than I thought," Brian said to his brother Michael. "She's always been one to keep her feelings all bottled up, but that's the only explanation. Mum must have meant a lot more to her than I ever knew."

"Or else it's guilt," said Michael, whose fiancée's sister was married to a man whose brother was a psychotherapist.

"Guilt? You have to be joking. What's she got to be guilty about? She couldn't have done more if she'd been Mum's own daughter."

"Yeah, but folks feel guilt over nothing when someone dies. It's a well-known fact."

"It is, is it? Is that what it is, doctor? Well, let me tell you something. If anyone ought to feel guilt, it's me. I've never said a word about this to a soul. Well, I couldn't, could I, not if I wanted to collect the insurance, but the fact is it was me set that place on fire."

"You what?" said Michael.

"It was an accident. I don't mean on purpose. Come on, what do you take me for, my own brother? And I don't feel guilty, I can tell you, I don't feel a scrap of guilt, accidents will happen and there's not a thing you can do about it. But when I went in to see Mum that afternoon I left my cigarette burning on the side of the chest of drawers. You know how you put them down, with the burning end stuck out. Linda'd taken away the damned ashtray and washed it or something. When I saw Mum was asleep I just crept out. Just crept out and left that fag end burning. Without a backward glance.''

Awed, Michael asked in a small voice, "When did you realize?''

"Soon as I saw the smoke, soon as I saw the fire brigade. Too late then, wasn't it? I'd crept out of there without a backward glance.''

THE CARER

The house and the people were new to her. They had given her a key, as most did. Angela had a cat to feed and a rubber plant to water. These tasks done, she went upstairs, feeling excited, and into the bedroom where she supposed they slept.

They had left it very tidy, the bed made with the covers drawn tight, everything on the dressing table neatly arranged. She opened the cupboards and had a look at their clothes. Then she examined the contents of the dressing-table drawers. A box of jewelry, scarves, handkerchiefs that no one used anymore. Another drawer was full of face creams and cosmetics. In the last one was a bundle of letters, tied up with pink ribbon. Angela untied the ribbon and read the letters, which were from Nigel to Maria, the people who lived here, love letters written before they were married and full of endearments, pet names, and promises of what he would do to her next time they met and how he expected she would respond.

She read them again before tying the ribbon around them and putting them back. Letters were a treat; she rarely came upon any in her explorations of other people's houses. Letters, like so many other things, had gone out of fashion. She went downstairs again, repeating under her breath some of the phrases Nigel had written and savoring them.

In the street where she lived Angela was much in demand as baby-sitter, dog-walker, cat-feeder, and general carer. Her clients, as she called them, thought her absolutely reliable and trustworthy. No one had ever suspected that she explored their houses while alone in them. After all, it had never occurred to Peter and Louise to place hairs across drawer handles, Elizabeth would hardly have known how to examine objects for fingerprints, Miriam and George were not observant people. Besides, they trusted her.

Angela lived alone in the house that had been her parents' and spent one weekend a month staying with her aunt in the Cotswolds, and while there she went to the Methodist church on Sunday. She had a job in the bank half a mile away. Once a year she and another single woman she had met at work went to Torquay or Bournemouth for a fortnight's holiday. She had never been out with a man; she never met any men except the ones in the street who were married or living with a partner. She had no real friends. She knitted, she read a lot, she slept ten hours a night.

Sometimes she asked herself how she had come to this way of living, why her life had not followed the pattern of other women's, why it had been without adventure or even event, but she could only answer that this was the way it had happened. Gradually it had happened without her seeing an alternative or knowing how to stop its inexorable progress to what it had become. Until, that is, Humphrey asked her to feed the cat while he was away and from that beginning she built up her business.

She had keys to eleven houses. Caring for them, their owners' children, elderly parents, pets, and plants, had become her only paid employment, for thankful to do so at last, she had given up her job. At first, performing these tasks punctually and efficiently had been enough, the gratitude she received and the payment. She liked her neighbors' dependence on her. She had become indispensable, and that gave her pleasure. But after a time she had grown restless sitting in John and Julia's living room with a sleeping baby upstairs; she had felt frustrated as she locked Humphrey's door and went home after feeding the cat. There should be something more, though more what? One night, when Diana's baby cried and she had been in to quieten it, her footsteps, as if independently of her will, took her along the passage into its parents' bedroom. And so it began.

The contents of cupboards and drawers, the bank statements and bills, Louise's diary that was her most prized find, Ken's certificates, Miriam's diplomas, Peter's prospectuses, Diana's holiday snapshots, all this showed her what life was. That it was the life of other people and not hers did not much trouble her. It educated her. Searching for it, finding new aspects of it, additions to what had been examined and learned before, was something to look forward to. There had not been much looking forward in her existence, or much looking back, come to that.

The neighbor who had written the love letters had recently moved into the house four doors down. She was recommended to him and his wife by Rose and Ken next door.

"If you'd like to let me have a key," Angela had said, "it will be quite safe with me." She made the little joke she always made. "I keep all the keys under lock and key."

"We're away quite a lot," said Maria, and Nigel said, "It

would be a load off our minds if we could rely on you to feed Absalom.''

When her business first started, Angela conducted her investigations of someone else's property only when legitimately there with a duty to perform. But after a while she became bolder and entered a house whenever the fancy took her. She would watch to see when her neighbors went out. Most of them were out at work all day anyway. It was true that all the keys were kept locked up. They were in a strongbox, each one labeled. Angela always asked for the back-door key. She said it was more convenient if there was a pet to be fed and perhaps exercised. What she didn't say was that you were less likely to be seen entering a house by the back door than the front.

The principal bedroom at Nigel and Maria's had been thoroughly explored on her first visit. But only that one bedroom. Once, greedy for sensation, during a single two-hour duty at John and Julia's she had searched every room, but since then she had learned restraint. It was something to dread, that the treasures in all the houses she had keys to might become exhausted, every secret laid bare, her gold mines overworked and left barren. So she had left the desk in Maria's living room for another time, though it had been almost more than she could bear, seeing it there, virgin so to speak, inviolate. She had left the desk untouched and all the cupboards and filing cabinets unplundered in the study they had made out of the third bedroom.

Maria went away one evening. Nigel told Angela she had gone and he would be joining her in a day or two. She noticed he stayed away from work and she waited for him to call and ask her to feed Absalom in his absence. He never came. Angela was much occupied with child-sitting for

Peter and Louise, driving Elizabeth's mother to the hospital, letting in the meter man and the plumber for Miriam and George, and taking Humphrey's cat to the vet, but she had time to wonder why he hadn't asked.

Returning home from watering Julia's peperomias, she met Nigel unlocking his car. He had Absalom with him in a wicker basket.

"Going away tonight?" Angela said hopefully.

"I shall be joining Maria. We thought we'd try taking Absalom with us this time, so we shan't require your kind services. But I expect you've plenty to do, haven't you?"

Thinking of the evening ahead, Angela said she had. She was almost as excited as on the day she began reading Louise's diary. Angela gave it an hour after Nigel's car had gone. She took the key out of the strongbox and let herself into the house. A happy two hours were spent in a search of the desk, and although it uncovered no more love letters, it did disclose several final demands for payment of bills, an angry note from George complaining about Absalom's behavior in his garden, and best of all, an anonymous letter.

This letter was printed in ink and suggested that Maria had been having an affair with someone called William. Angela thought about this and wondered what it would be like—having an affair when you were married, that is—and she wondered what being married was like anyway, and whether it was William's wife or girlfriend who had written the letter. She put everything back in the desk just as she had found it, being careful not to tidy up.

The rooms upstairs she left for next day. It was a Friday and she was due to drive to Auntie Joan's for the weekend that evening, but first she had Elizabeth's dogs to walk morning and afternoon and Elizabeth's mother to fetch from the hospital, the electrician to let in for Rose and Ken, and Louise's little girl to meet from school. There were two hours to spare between coming back from the hospital and fetching Alexandra. Taking care not to be seen by the electrician, putting in a new outlet next door in the back room, Angela let herself into Nigel and Maria's house.

Overnight she had felt rather nervous about that desk, and the first thing she did was check that everything was back in place. An examination quickly reassured her that she had accurately replicated their untidiness. Then she went upstairs and along the passage to the study. Louise's diary notwithstanding, Maria and Nigel's house promised to afford her the richest seam of treasure she had yet encountered. And who knew what would be behind this door in the cupboards and the filing cabinets? More love letters, perhaps, hers to him this time, more insinuations of Maria's infidelity, more unpaid bills, even something pointing to illegality or crime.

Angela opened the door. She took a step into the room, then a step backward, uttering a small scream she would have suppressed if she could. Maria lay on the floor, wearing a nightdress, her long hair loose and spread out. There was a large brown stain that must be blood on the front of her nightdress and unmistakable blood on the floor around her. Angela stood still for what seemed a very long time, holding her hand over her mouth. She forced herself to advance upon Maria and touch her. It was her forehead she touched, white as marble. Her fingertip encountered icy coldness, and she pulled it away with a shudder. Maria's dead eyes looked at her, round and blue like marbles.

Angela went quickly downstairs. She was trembling all over. She let herself out the back door, locked the door, and put the key through the letter box at the front. It somehow seemed essential to her not to have that key in her possession.

She went home and packed a bag, found her car keys. Fetching Alexandra was forgotten, and so were Elizabeth's dogs. Angela got into her car and drove off northward, exceeding the speed limit within the first five minutes. She thought she would stay at least a fortnight with Auntie Joan. Perhaps she would never come back at all. If this was life, they could keep it. It was death, too.

THE MAN WHO WAS THE GOD OF LOVE

"Have you got the *Times* there?" Henry would say, usually at about eight, when she had cleared the dinner table and put the things in the dishwasher.

The *Times* was on the coffee table with the two other dailies they took, but it was part of the ritual to ask her. Fiona liked to be asked. She liked to watch Henry do the crossword puzzle—the *real* one of course, not the quick crossword—and watch him frown a little, his handsome brow clear as the answer to a clue came to him. She could not have done a crossword puzzle to save her life (as she was fond of saying); she could not even have done the simple ones in the tabloids.

While she watched him, before he carried the newspaper off into his study as he often did, Fiona told herself how lucky she was to be married to Henry. Her luck had been almost miraculous. There she was, a temp who had come into his office to work for him while his secretary had a baby, an ordinary, not particularly good-looking girl who had no credentials but a tidy mind and a proficient way with a word processor. She had nothing but her admiration for him, which she had felt from the first and was quite unable to hide.

He was not appreciated in that company as he should have been. It had often seemed to her that only she saw him for what he was. After she had been there a week she told him he had a first-class mind.

Henry had said modestly, "As a matter of fact, I have got rather a high IQ, but it doesn't exactly get stretched round here."

"I suppose they haven't the brains to recognize it," she said. "It must be marvelous to be really intelligent. Did you win scholarships and get a double first and all that?"

He only smiled. Instead of answering he asked her to have dinner with him. One afternoon, half an hour before they were due to pack up and go, she came upon him doing the *Times* crossword.

"In the firm's time, I'm afraid, Fiona," he said with one of his wonderful, half-rueful smiles.

He hadn't finished the puzzle, but at least half of it was already filled in and when she asked him he said he had started it ten minutes before. She was lost in admiration. Henry said he would finish the puzzle later and in the meantime would she have a drink with him on the way home?

That was three years ago. The firm, which deserved bankruptcy it was so mismanaged, got into difficulties and Henry was among those made redundant. Of course, he soon got another job, though the salary was pitiful for someone of his intellectual grasp. He was earning very little more than she was, as she told him indignantly. Soon afterward he asked her to marry him. Fiona was overcome. She told him humbly that she would have gladly lived with him without marriage, there was no one else she had ever known to compare with him in intellectual terms, it would have been enough to be allowed to share his life. But he said no, marriage or nothing, it would be unfair on her not to marry her.

She kept on with her temping job, making sure she stopped in time to be home before Henry and get his dinner. It was ridiculous to waste money on a cleaner, so she cleaned the house on Sundays. Henry played golf on Saturday mornings and he liked her to go with him, though she was hopeless when she tried to learn. He said it was an inspiration to have her there and praise his swing. On Saturday afternoons they went out in the car, and Henry had begun teaching her to drive.

They had quite a big garden—they had bought the house on an enormous mortgage—and she did her best to keep it trim, because Henry obviously didn't have the time. He was engaged on a big project for his new company that he worked on in his study for most of the evenings. Fiona did the shopping in her lunchtime; she did all the cooking and all the washing and ironing. It was her privilege to care for someone as brilliant as Henry. Besides, his job was so much more demanding than hers it took more out of him, and by bedtime he was sometimes white with exhaustion.

But Henry was first up in the mornings. He was an early riser, getting up at six-thirty, and he always brought her a cup of tea and the morning papers in bed. Fiona had nothing to do before she went off to take first a bus and then the tube but put the breakfast things in the dishwasher and stack yesterday's newspapers in the cupboard outside the front door for recycling.

The *Times* would usually be on top, folded with the lower left-hand quarter of the back page uppermost.

Fiona soon came to understand it was no accident that the section of the paper where the crossword was, the *completed* crossword, should be exposed in this way. It was deliberate, it was evidence of Henry's pride in his achievement, and she was deeply moved that he should want her to see it. She was touched by his need for her admiration. A sign of weakness on his part it might be, but she loved him all the more for that.

A smile, half admiring, half tender, came to her lips, as she looked at the neatly printed answers to all those incomprehensible clues. She could have counted on the fingers of one hand the number of times he had failed to finish the crossword. The evening before his father died, for instance. Then it was anxiety that must have been the cause. They had sent for him at four in the morning, and when she looked at the paper before putting it outside with the others, she saw that poor Henry had only been able to fill in the answers to four clues. Another time he had flu and had been unable to get out of bed in the morning. It must have been coming on the night before, to judge by his attempt at the crossword, abandoned after two answers feebly penciled in.

His father left him a house that was worth a lot of money. Henry had always said that when he got promotion, she would be able to give up work and have a baby. Promotion seemed less and less likely in time of recession and in view of the fact that the new company appreciated Henry no more than had his previous employers. The proceeds of the sale of Henry's father's house would compensate for that, and Fiona was imagining paying off the mortgage and perhaps handing in her notice when Henry said he was going to spend it on having a swimming pool built. All his life he had wanted a swimming pool of his own; it had been a childhood dream and a teenage ideal, and now he was going to realize it.

Fiona came nearer than she ever had to seeing a flaw in her husband's perfection.

"You only want a baby because you think he might be a genius," he teased her.

"*She* might be," said Fiona, greatly daring.

"He, she, it's just a manner of speaking. Suppose he had my beauty and your brains. That would be a fine turnup for the books."

Fiona was not hurt, because she had never had any illusions about being brighter than she was. In any case, he was implying, wasn't he, that she was good-looking? She managed to laugh. She understood that Henry could not always help being rather difficult. It was the penalty someone like him paid for his gifts of brilliance. In some ways intellectual prowess was a burden to carry through life.

"We'll have a heated pool, a decent-size one with a deep end," Henry said, "and I'll teach you to swim."

The driving lessons had ended in failure. If it had been anyone else but Henry instructing her, Fiona would have said he was a harsh and intolerant teacher. Of course, she knew how inept she was. She could not learn how to manage the gears and she was afraid of the traffic.

"I'm afraid of the water," she confessed.

"It's a disgrace," he said as if she had not spoken, "a woman of thirty being unable to swim." And then, when she only nodded doubtfully, "Have you got the *Times* there?"

❑   ❑   ❑

Building the pool took all the money the sale of Henry's father's house realized. It took rather more, and Henry had to borrow from the bank. The pool had a roof over it and walls around, which were what cost the money. That and the sophisticated purifying system. It was eight feet deep at the deep end, with a diving board and a slide.

Happily for Fiona, her swimming lessons were indefinitely postponed. Henry enjoyed his new pool so much that he would very much have grudged taking time off from swimming his lengths or practicing his dives in order to teach his wife the basics.

Fiona guessed that Henry would be a brilliant swimmer. He was the perfect all-arounder. There was an expression in Latin that he had uttered and then translated for her, which might have been, she thought, a description of himself: *mens sana in corpore sano.* Only for *"sana,"* or "healthy," she substituted "wonderful." She would have liked to sit by the pool and watch him, and she was rather sorry that his preferred swimming time was six-thirty in the morning, long before she was up.

One evening, while doing the crossword puzzle, he consulted her about a clue, as he sometimes did. "Consulted" was not perhaps the word. It was more a matter of expressing his thoughts aloud and waiting for her comment. Fiona found these remarks, full of references to unknown classical or literary personages, nearly incomprehensible. She had heard, for instance, of Psyche but only in connection with "psychological," "psychiatric," and so on. Cupid to her was a fat baby with wings, and she did not know this was another name for Eros, which to her was the statue.

"I'm afraid I don't understand at all," she said humbly.

Henry loved elucidating. With a rare gesture of affection, he reached out and squeezed her hand. "Psyche was married to Cupid, who was, of course, a god, the god of love. He always came to her by night and she never saw his face. Suppose her husband was a terrible monster of ugliness and deformity? Against his express wishes"—here Henry fixed a look of some severity on his wife—"she rose up one night in the dark and, taking a lighted candle, approached the bed where Cupid lay. Scarcely had she caught a glimpse of his peerless beauty, when a drop of hot wax fell from the candle onto the god's naked skin. With a cry he sprang up and fled from the house. She never saw him again."

"That's so sad."

"Yes, well, she shouldn't have disobeyed him. Still, I don't see how that quite fits in here—wait a minute, yes, I do. Of course, that second syllable is an anagram on Eros . . ."

Henry inserted the letters in his neat print. A covert glance told her he had completed nearly half the puzzle. She did her best to suppress a yawn. By this time of the evening she was always so tired she could scarcely keep awake, while Henry could stay up for hours yet. People like him needed no more than four or five hours' sleep.

"I think I'll go up," she said.

"Good night." He added a kindly "darling."

For some reason, Henry never did the crossword puzzle on a Saturday. Fiona thought this a pity because, as she said, that was the day they gave prizes for the first correct entries received. But Henry only smiled and said he did the puzzle for the pure intellectual pleasure of it, not for gain. Of course, you might not know your entry was correct because the solution to Saturday's puzzle did not appear next day but not until a week later. Her saying this, perhaps naively, made Henry unexpectedly angry. Everyone knew that with this kind of puzzle, he said, there could only be one correct solution; even people who never did crosswords knew that.

It was still dark when Henry got up in the mornings. Sometimes she was aware of his departure and his empty half of the bed. Occasionally, half an hour later, she heard the boy come with the papers, the tap-tap of the letterbox and even the soft thump of the *Times* falling onto the mat. But most days she was aware of nothing until Henry reappeared with her tea and the papers.

Henry did nothing to make her feel guilty about lying in, yet she was ashamed of her inability to get up. It was somehow unlike him, it was out of character, this waiting on her. He never did anything of the kind at any other time of the day, and it sometimes seemed to her that the unselfish effort he made must be almost intolerable to someone with his needle-sharp mind and—yes, it must be admitted—his undoubted lack of patience. That he never complained or even teased her about oversleeping only added to her guilt.

Shopping in her lunch hour, she bought an alarm clock. They had never possessed such a thing, had never needed to, for Henry, as he often said, could direct himself to wake up at any hour he chose. Fiona put the alarm clock inside her bedside cabinet where it was invisible. It occurred to her, although she had as yet done nothing—she had not set the clock—that in failing to tell Henry about her purchase of the alarm she was deceiving him. This was the first time she had ever deceived him in anything, and perhaps, as she reflected on this, it was inevitable that her thoughts should revert to Cupid and Psyche and the outcome of Psyche's equally innocent stratagem.

The alarm remained inside the cabinet. Every evening she thought of setting it, though she never did so. But the effect on her of this daily speculation and doubt was to wake her without benefit of mechanical aid. Thinking about it did the trick, and Henry, in swimming trunks and toweling robe, had no sooner left their bedroom than she was wide awake. On the third morning this happened, instead of dozing off again until seven-thirty, she lay there for ten minutes and then got up.

Henry would be swimming his lengths. She heard the paperboy come, the letterbox make its double tap-tap, and the newspapers fall onto the mat with a soft thump. Should she put on her own swimming costume or go down fully dressed? Finally, she compromised and got into the tracksuit that had never seen a track and scarcely the light of day before.

This morning it would be she who made Henry tea and took *him* the papers. However, when she reached the foot of the stairs there was no paper on the mat, only a brown envelope with a bill in it. She must have been mistaken and it was the postman she had heard. The time was just on seven, rather too soon perhaps for the papers to have arrived.

Fiona made her way to the swimming pool. When she saw Henry she would just wave airily to him. She might call out in a cheerful way, "Carry on swimming!" or make some other humorous remark.

The glass door to the pool was slightly ajar. Fiona was barefoot. She pushed the door and entered silently. The cold chemical smell of chlorine irritated her nostrils. It was still dark outside, though dawn was coming, and the dark purplish blue of a presunrise sky shimmered through the glass panel in the ceiling. Henry was not in the pool but sitting in one of the cane chairs at the glass-topped table not two yards from her. Light from a ceiling spotlight fell directly onto the two newspapers in front of him, both folded with their back pages uppermost.

Fiona saw at once what he was doing. That was not the difficulty. From today's *Times* he was copying into yesterday's *Times* the answers to the crossword puzzle. She could see quite clearly that he was doing this but she could not for a moment believe. It must be a joke or there must be some other purpose behind it.

When he turned around, swiftly covering both newspapers with the *Radio Times,* she knew from his face that it was neither a joke nor the consequence of some mysterious purpose. He had turned quite white. He seemed unable to speak, and she flinched from the panic that leapt in his eyes.

"I'll make us a cup of tea," she said.

The wisest and kindest thing would be to forget what she had seen. She could not. In that split second she stood in the doorway of the pool watching him he had been changed forever in her eyes. She thought about it on and off all day. It was impossible for her to concentrate on her work.

She never once thought that he had deceived her, only that she had caught him. Like Psyche, she had held the candle over him and seen his true face. His was not the brilliant intellect she had thought. He could not even finish the *Times* crossword. Now she understood why he never attempted it on a Saturday, knowing there would be no opportunity next morning or on the Monday morning to fill in the answers from that day's paper. There were a lot of other truths that she saw about Henry. No one recognized his mind as first-class because it wasn't first-class. He had lost that excellent well-paid job because he was not intellectually up to it.

She knew all that and she loved him the more for it. Just as she had felt an almost maternal tenderness for him when he left the newspaper with its completed puzzle exposed for her to see, now she was overwhelmed with compassion for his weakness and his childlike vulnerability. She loved him more deeply than ever, and if admiration and respect had gone, what did those things matter, after all, in the tender intimacy of a good marriage?

That evening he did not touch the crossword puzzle. She had known he wouldn't, and of course she said nothing. Neither of them had said a word about what she had seen that morning and neither of them ever would. Her feelings for him were completely changed, yet she believed her attitude could remain unaltered. But when, a few days later, he said something more about its being disgraceful that a woman of her age was unable to swim, instead of agreeing ruefully, she laughed and said, really, he shouldn't be so intolerant and censorious, no one was perfect.

He gave her a complicated explanation of some monetary question that was raised on the television news. It sounded wrong—he was confusing dollars with pounds—and she said so.

"Since when have you been an expert on the stock market?" he said.

Once she would have apologized. "I'm no more an expert than you are, Henry," she said, "but I can use my eyes, and that was plain to see. Don't you think we should both admit we don't know a thing about it?"

She no longer believed in the accuracy of his translations

from the Latin or the authenticity of his tales from the classics. When some friends who came for dinner were regaled with his favorite story about how she had been unable to learn to drive, she jumped up laughing and put her arm around his shoulder.

"Poor Henry gets into a rage so easily I was afraid he'd give himself a heart attack, so I stopped our lessons," she said.

He never told that story again.

"Isn't it funny?" she said one Saturday on the golf course. "I used to think it was wonderful, you having a handicap of twenty-five. I didn't know any better."

He made no answer.

"It's not really the best thing in a marriage for one partner to look up to the other too much, is it? Equality is best. I suppose it's natural to idolize the other one when you're first married. It just went on rather a long time for me, that's all."

She was no longer in the least nervous about learning to swim. If he bullied her she would laugh at him. As a matter of fact, he wasn't all that good a swimmer himself. He couldn't do the crawl at all, and a good many of his dives turned into belly flops. She lay on the side of the pool, leaning on her elbows, watching him as he climbed out of the deep end up the steps.

"D'you know, Henry," she said, "you'll lose your marvelous figure if you aren't careful. You've got quite a spare tire round your waist."

His face was such a mask of tragedy, there was so much naked misery there, the eyes full of pain, that she checked the laughter that was bubbling up in her and said quickly, "Oh, don't look so sad, poor darling. I'd still love you if you were as fat as a pudding and weighed twenty stone.''

He took two steps backward down the steps, put up his hands, and pulled her down into the pool. It happened so quickly and unexpectedly that she didn't resist. She gasped when the water hit her. It was eight feet deep here, she couldn't swim more than two or three strokes, and she made a grab for him, clutching at his upper arms.

He prized her fingers open and pushed her under the water. She tried to scream, but the water came in and filled her throat. Desperately she thrashed about it in the blue-greenness, the sickeningly chlorinated water, fighting, sinking, feeling for something to catch hold of, the bar around the pool rim, his arms, his feet on the steps. A foot kicked out at her, a foot stamped on her head. She stopped holding her breath, she had to, and the water poured into her lungs until the light behind her eyes turned red and her head was black inside. A great drumbeat, boom, boom, boom, in the blackness, and then it stopped.

Henry waited to see if the body would float to the surface. He waited a long time, but she remained, starfishlike, face-downward, on the blue tiles eight feet down, so he left her and, wrapping himself in his toweling robe, went into the house. Whatever happened, whatever steps if any he decided to take next, he would do the *Times* crossword that evening. Or as much of it as he could ever do.

EXPECTATIONS

No varnish can hide the grain of the wood, as my cousin
Matthew once said of my late husband, adding that no man
who was not a true gentleman at heart ever was a true gentleman in manner. George, however, succeeded in passing
himself off as well-born and well-educated, and in recent
years it had only been his wife and daughter who knew the
real man behind the smile and the black clothes and those
snow-white pocket handkerchiefs. Only I and Estella knew
the criminality hidden under the mellifluous speech-mak-
ing and verse-quoting and his handsome looks.

But a gentleman who is upright and admirable is not
found stabbed to death on Epsom racecourse as George was
three weeks ago. A man as virtuous as some of his acquaintance believed him to be does not leave on his death a con-
tented widow and a joyful daughter. The truth is that,
shocked as I was when the news of his murder was brought
to me, I was also relieved. These twenty years gone by have
sometimes been almost intolerable—though what course is
there for a woman but to tolerate?—and George's death,
horrible though the circumstances of it were, lifted the load
from my shoulders in the twinkling of an eye.

His grave is in our village churchyard. Living in London,

I missed the countryside and longed to go back. The brewery and all the property, of course, became George's on our marriage. I only deceive myself if I deny that it was to possess them that George married me, but I am glad he kept Satis House, in spite of disliking it so thoroughly. I have returned to it and am about to take my place in county society with my daughter, who comes out in a year's time. By then my mourning will be over and I shall give a ball for her. There will be some hearts broken when the young blades thereabouts set eyes on Estella. Her very name means a star. I always vowed that if I had a girl she should be called Estella, and George for once put up no opposition. He, of course, wanted a son.

She is far more beautiful than I ever was. She is tall like her father and has his dark, curly hair. It is extraordinary to me now the effect he had upon me when Arthur brought him home to meet me all those years ago. I fell in love with him that first evening. But even then, blind as I was to everything but George's beauty and George's grace, I retained sense enough to wonder why my half sibling—I will not dignify Arthur with the name of brother—was so desirous that his friend should like me and I return that particular regard.

Arthur was envious because our father left the greater part of his property to me, his elder child. Perhaps I should have reminded him more often that his riotous and undutiful behavior almost secured him disinheritance. It was only on his deathbed that Papa relented and left him a share in the brewery. But that and the income which came with it was insufficient for Arthur, as I soon understood, though it was not until just before my marriage that I knew of the conspiracy got up between him and George.

Should I have refused George money? Would a prudent young woman have refused? I was so afraid to lose him. Of course, I had suitors enough, but I wanted none of them. I wanted George. And the truth of what he said to me was undeniable.

"Why not a thousand pounds now, my dearest, bearing in mind that it will all be mine once we are married? Mine to husband for you and watch over diligently when you are my wife?"

So I agreed. Then, and again and again.

Three weeks before our wedding George was staying in the house, and one night, unable to sleep, I came downstairs to find myself a book from the library. They were inside, Arthur and George, sitting over the dying fire with, no doubt, the brandy bottle. The door was a little ajar and I heard their voices.

I had been so certain they would have retired by now that I had come down in my nightgown with only a shawl thrown about me. So I paused at the door, uncertain of what to do next. Then I heard Arthur say,

"She shall have my share of the brewery, my boy, but I'll want a great sum for it, so mind you tell her not to jib at the price."

George laughed. "I'm likely to do that, am I? What, when you and I are dividing the sum between us?"

The man I had been used to call my brother said, "You'll be off then, Compeyson, will you?"

"Don't speak so loud." George's voice was almost too low for me to hear. "The long and the short of it is that I'll only marry her if she won't buy you out. But she will, she will. Why, she's so much in love she'd follow me to the ends of the earth in her petticoat."

It was true. But I trembled as I stood there, drawing the ends of the shawl about me, returning to bed slowly, moving like a sleepwalker. There was no sleep for me that night. I had no one to advise me, though I knew, ignorant as I was, what advice the wise would give. But I loved him. In spite of his treachery, I loved him. I saw the grain through the varnish but still I loved him.

Next day and the next and the next George pleaded with me. When he was my husband, he said, it was only fitting that he should hold the brewery and manage it all. For a while I played the same game he played. I asked Arthur's price and pretended to be appalled at the sum. I counted the days to our wedding day, nineteen days, then eighteen days. My clothes were bought; I had had three fittings for my wedding gown. George said all that would be needful was for me to sign a paper he would bring me.

Over the first paper I succeeded in spilling ink. Fifteen days, fourteen. I sent to the town for an attorney. He came and looked at the paper, he took it away with him and the days passed, thirteen, twelve, eleven, but he returned with the paper and pronounced it a legal document. There was no obstacle to my signing it. Except myself. I took my courage in my hands and told George I would be happiest to have *him* buy Arthur out, that I was a mere woman and unfit for business. Once we were married he would have an ample sum with which to purchase Arthur's share.

That was six days before the wedding. George was gone and I saw and heard nothing of him. I had no sleep; I could scarcely rest. But the wedding dress was finished and the bride-cake made and at last the day of my marriage came. Arthur was to give me away, but I had heard nothing of Arthur. George was to be my husband, and I had received no sign from him for a week.

It was twenty minutes to nine in the morning and I was seated at my dressing table in front of a gilded looking glass. My maid had dressed me in satin and lace, all white, and put bridal flowers in my hair and Mama's diamonds about my neck. Half-packed trunks stood about the room. I remember the moment when the note came. My veil was on but half arranged, and I had but one shoe on, the other being on the table near my hand with trinkets and gloves and a Prayer Book and some flowers, all confusedly heaped about the looking glass.

My maid came in and put the note into my hand. Time and the whole world seemed to stop, and I thought, If this letter tells me he is gone time shall indeed stop and I will remain forever in this moment. I will wear this dress for the rest of my life, with one shoe off and one on, until my hair is white and my skin is yellow. The feast shall remain spread until dust covers it and the bride-cake be a nest for spiders to veil with their webs.

I opened George's letter. "My dearest," he wrote, and he went on to say he loved me, he had been unavoidably absent these past days but he would be awaiting me in the church. I let my maid arrange my veil, I put on my shoe, the rings on my fingers and then the gloves. I took up the flowers and the Prayer Book and descended the stairs to meet Arthur at the foot and have him take me to be married.

Love was faded within the year. The varnish was stripped away and I saw only the grain, but yet I was married, I was Mrs. George Compeyson with the dignity of a wife. I had my child to watch grow in health and beauty. Satis House, the name that means a sufficiency, awaited me for my widow-hood, and they used to say, when the name was given, that whoever had that house could want nothing else. Enough of my fortune remains after George's depredations for me to live in comfort and give Estella twenty thousand pounds on her marriage.

If I sometimes feel a little low and see myself growing old, my life wasted, I go into that room that was once my bedchamber and sit at the dressing table. There, staring into the looking glass, I tell myself to be thankful for what I did and what I did not do, for a year of love and a lovely child, and that I am not still in that white dress and veil, one shoe off and one shoe on, doomed to be forever Miss Havisham.

SHREDS AND SLIVERS

I love my love with a *ps* because she is psychic; I hate her with a *ps* because she is psilotic. I feed her on psalliota and psilotaceae; her name is Psammis and she lives in a psalterium.

Forgive me. I am carried away by words sometimes, especially those of Greek etymology that begin with a combination of unlikely consonants. I love my love with a *cn* because she is cnidarian. . . . But, no. Let us return to psalliota. If you want to know what all those other words mean you must look them up in a good dictionary. Psalliota is nothing more nor less than the common mushroom: *Psalliota campestris,* to be precise.

I became interested in fungi only recently. Since being made redundant I have, of course, had time on my hands, leisure to notice things. I try not to brood. That this year was exceptional for an abundance of fungi first struck me while taking a train to see my wife. I can no longer afford to run a car. From the economy-class window I observed meadows covered with whitish protrusions among the grass. It took me only a little while to realize that these were mushrooms, though I had never seen such a sight before.

Back at home after my day out, I explored my garden.

Largely untended (I sometimes mow the lawn) since my wife was stolen from me ten years ago, it has gone back to nature in rather a pleasing way. For instance, shrubs that she planted have transformed themselves into trees. Under them and in mossy corners against the walls, I came upon a variety of fungi: agarics, lepiotas, horns of plenty, and, of course, the puffball. These names were unfamiliar to me then. Two books and a video started me on what may become a lifelong obsession.

I am not a mushroom eater myself. My wife was particularly fond of them. But in those days—I won't say when I last saw her, for I make a point of *seeing* her, but when I last spoke to her—the only mushrooms obtainable in the shops were the common kind, and the only differentiation that between "large" and "button." Things have changed. To the uninitiated these supermarket cartons, wrapped in cling film, may appear to contain only "mixed mushrooms"; I, however, can name them as shiitaki, canterelles, boletus, and morels, pale slivers resembling slices of blood-drained flesh, lemony fibrous strips, plump glutinous gobbets, chocolate-brown elastic lumps. Well, there is no accounting for tastes.

The day I came upon *Amanita phalloides* in my garden, under the Sessile oak, was the day I saw my wife for the first time in some weeks. You understand that though I think about her every day, go to the town where she lives, keep an eye on her house, and spend some time in her local shopping center, I do not always see her. Needless to say, she *never* sees me. But on this occasion, invisible among the racks of shellsuits, I spotted her in the distance approaching the vegetable counters. I am not exaggerating when I say my heart quaked. It is always a shock, even after so long.

90

I watched from my sartorial hideaway. Too far away to see what she bought, I followed her with my eyes from vegetables to pizzas, from pasta to mineral waters, and thence to the checkout. That night I ran the video through once again. Yellow and white, with pallid gills and raggedy hat, phalloides blossomed on the screen in all its deadly glory. The Death Cap, as the voice-over called it, adding cheerfully that very small quantities cause intense suffering, then death.

If I were to grow *Cannabis sativa* I would be breaking the law. The police would come, root up and destroy the plants. But it is no offense to grow phalloides, most deadly of all indigenous fungi. With impunity, I might if I wished turn my shady half-acre into a Death Cap plantation. If only I could! But fungi are capricious, inconstant; fungi are fitful and vicissitudinous. Who has not heard of those would-be mushroom farmers who have the kit and precisely obey the instructions, only to find their growing barns empty and psalliota flourishing in the fields outside their property?

I have had to be content with what nature has supplied, and for my part can provide only encouragement in the form of shade, moisture, and protection. It was in October that the young fruit first broke through and the stipe pushed above the ground, its snowy veil bursting to reveal the olive-yellow cap. The flesh, my book says, is white and smells of raw potatoes. How gratifying to discover that this was indeed so and I had not confused phalloides with, for instance, xerula. (I love my love with an *x* because she is xanthic; I hate her with an *x* because she is xylophagous.)

Careful not to touch the fruit bodies, using a knife and fork, I sliced into thin strips the cap and stipe of three specimens. They filled a large yogurt pot. With closed eyes, I stood there remembering my wife's ways, her fashion of cooking, her pleasure in eating, her smile. I remembered her slicing raw potatoes and I could smell the smell in my mind.

I took the yogurt pot with me next day and went straight from the station to the supermarket. There was no question of my wife's arriving for at least two hours; I have my memories, all too many of them, and I know her timetable, the order and regularity of her life. But for a while I waited, pacing, deep in thought, between bed-linen reductions and kitchenware. You must appreciate that until then, apart from the audiotapes and the carefully chosen articles sent her, and the enlightening letters posted to her relatives, I had taken no positive steps against my wife. The time had come for action. I hesitated no longer.

With a little practice, it takes only seconds to detach the cling film from the base of a mixed mushroom carton, slip in a slice or two of phalloides, and readhere the film. Among the fronds and filaments, the shreds and slivers, my delicate cilia passed unnoticed or passed for wisps of shiitaki. I operated on some ten cartons, about half the stock, in this way. The place was not frequented at lunchtime. No one saw me, or if they did, approved the prudence of what they took for close examination prior to purchase. I have noticed how, for example, in these hard times, it is not uncommon for shoppers to taste the grapes before they buy.

I waited long enough to see my wife come in. My heart began to jog. One day, if this does not stop, it will kill itself and me with it. Of course, I realized that there was only a fifty percent chance of my wife consuming one of the fatal batch. But in this game of culinary Russian roulette, these are very favorable odds. Still, on my next visit with fresh supplies I operated on fifteen cartons. After all, she is not the only one to consider but also her live-in paramour and her extended family, who all live nearby and whose sheepish faces and obese forms I often see in the aisles between the sauces and the frozen desserts.

At last, having heard and seen nothing of the consequence of my actions, I was obliged to sacrifice the last of the phalloides, stripping the leaf mold under the Sessile oak bare of its potato-scented crop. This time—I was a little late—only fourteen cartons of mixed mushrooms remained, and in less than two minutes the contents of the yogurt pot were nestling among the sinuate gills and elliptoid membranes. In fact, I had barely finished when I spotted her entering by way of exotic fruits and, my heart on its treadmill, I slipped away.

Three days later a small paragraph in the newspaper told me that the supermarket had withdrawn all "mixed mushrooms" due to two unexplained deaths and several cases of severe illness. But the deaths, alas, were not hers nor his nor theirs. When it has blown over and "mixed mushrooms" are back on the counter, I shall have to begin all over again next year.

At present the ground under the Sessile oak is covered with snow. All fungi have succumbed to frost. I shall mark the spot where the spores of phalloides lie deep in the earth, for there must be no trampling or digging. And some mnemonic must be contrived to help me remember the precise location. Oh, I love my love with an *mn* because she is mnemic, I hate her with an *mn* because she is mnemonical; her name is Mnemosyne and she is the goddess of remembrance. . . .

CLOTHES

"I'd like this, please."

She had put the dress down on the counter. The look the assistant gave her was slightly apprehensive. Alison had sounded breathless; she had sounded elated. Now that it was too late, she restrained herself.

"How would you like to pay?"

Instead of answering, she laid the credit card on the counter where the dress was now being folded, amid layers of tissue paper. The bill came waving out of the machine and she signed in the too-small space on the right-hand side. At this point, and it was always the same, she couldn't wait to get away. Lingering, chatting to the assistant— "You'll get a lot of wear out of this one," "Enjoy wearing it"—embarrassed her. She felt as if she was there on false pretenses or as if her secret self must inevitably be revealed. She walked off quickly and she was happy; she felt the familiar buzz, the swing of lightheadedness, the rush of adrenaline. She had made her day; she had bought something.

Once outside, she took the dress out of the bag and put it into her briefcase, along with the outline plans for the Grimwood project. That way the people in the office would not know what she had been doing. The carrier went into a litter bin and the bill with it. A taxi came and she got into it. Already the level of excitement had begun to flag. By the time she walked into the PR consultancy of which she was chief executive none of it was left. She smiled and told her assistant lunch had gone on longer than expected.

On the way home she bought something else. She didn't mean to. But that went without saying, for she scarcely ever did mean to. It was where she lived, she sometimes thought, the dangerous place she lived in, Knightsbridge, shopping country. If she and Gil moved, out into the sticks, some distant suburb . . . She knew they wouldn't.

She should have taken a taxi to her doorstep, not used the tube. Some of it was the fault of the dress, for now she knew she disliked the dress, the color, the cut. She would never wear it, and the amount she had spent on it printed itself on her mind in black letters. The elation it had brought her had turned to panic. Absurdly, she had taken the tube to save money, because it cost ninety pence and a taxi would have been five pounds. But it gave her a half-mile walk down Sloane Street. At six, on late-closing night.

Sometimes Alison thought of the things she might have done at leisure in London. Gone to the National Gallery, the Wallace Collection, walked in the parks, joined the London Library. She had heard the Museum of the Moving Image was wonderful. Instead she went shopping. She bought things. Well, she bought clothes. Halfway down the long street of shops, her eye was caught by a sweater in a window. The feeling was familiar, the faint breathlessness, the drying mouth, the words repeated in her head—she must have it, she must have it. On these occasions she seemed to see the future so clearly. She seemed to live in advance the regret she would feel if she didn't have the thing, whatever it was. The remorse experienced when she *did* have it was forgotten.

The knob on the shop door was a heavy glass ball, set in brass. She closed her hand over the knob. She paused. But that was not unusual. Hesitating on the doorstep, she told herself she was buying this sweater because she had made a mistake with the dress. She didn't like the dress, but the sweater would make up for that. She turned the knob and the door came open. Inside a woman sat at a gilded table with a marble top. She lifted her head, smiled at Alison, and said, "Hi." Alison knew the woman wouldn't get up and come over and start showing her things; it wasn't that kind of shop, and Alison knew about shops. She went to the rack where the sweater and its fellows hung. The fever was already upon her and reason gone. This feeling was like a combination of sexual excitement and the effect of one strong drink. When it had her in its clutch she stopped thinking, or rather, she thought only of the garment before her: how it would look on her, where she would wear it and when, how possessing it would change her life for the better.

Shopping had to be done in a rush. That was part of the whole character of it. Do it fast and do it impulsively. The blood beat in her head. She took the sweater off its hanger, held it up against herself.

The woman said, "Would you like to try it on?"

"I'll have it," Alison said. She took an identical sweater off the rack, but in a darker shade. "In fact, I'll have both." She responded to the assistant's smile with a radiant smile of her own.

When she had paid and was outside the shop once more, she looked at her watch and saw that the whole transaction had taken seven minutes. The two sweaters were too bulky to go in the briefcase, so she took out the dress and put it in the black shiny white-lettered bag with her new purchases. She began to think of how she was going to get into the flat without Gil's seeing she had been shopping.

He might not be home yet. Sometimes he came in first, sometimes she did. If he was home she might be able to get into the bedroom and hide the bag before he saw. If worse came to worst and he saw the bag he would suppose there was only one garment inside it, not three. The buzz was easing up, the adrenaline was being absorbed, and she understood something else: this was the first time she had bought something without trying it on first.

The glass doors opened for her and she walked in. She went up in the lift. Her key slipped into the lock and turned and the front door opened. It was impossible to tell if he was there or not. She called out, "Gil?" and his voice answering from the kitchen, "I'm in here," made her jump. She ran into the bedroom and thrust the bag into the back of the clothes cupboard.

It was his evening to cook. She had forgotten. When she was shopping she forgot everything else. She went into the kitchen and put her arms around him and kissed him. He was wearing an apron and holding a wooden spoon.

"Tell me," he said. "Do you actually like dried tomatoes?"

"Dried tomatoes? I've never thought about it. Well, no, I don't suppose I do really."

"No one does. That's my great culinary discovery of the week. No one does but they pretend to, like they do about green peppers."

Gil enlarged on this. He produced a cookery program

for television and began telling her about a soufflé that kept going wrong. At the fourth attempt the star of the program, a temperamental man, had picked up and upended the spoiled soufflé over the head of one of the camera crew. Alison listened and laughed in the right places and told him about the latest developments in the Grimwood account. He said he'd give her a shout when the food was ready and she went away into the bedroom to change.

Every evening, if they weren't going out, she changed into jeans or tracksuit pants and a sweatshirt. The irony was that these were old, she had had them for years, while the cupboard groaned under the weight of new clothes. There was barely room for the new dress and the sweaters to squeeze in. When would she wear any of them? Perhaps never. Perhaps, unworn, they would join the stack that must soon be packed into her largest suitcase and be taken to the hospice shop.

They loved her in the hospice shop. They called her Alison, they knew her so well. "What lovely clothes you always bring us, Alison," and "You have quite a turnover in clothes, Alison—well, you must have in your job." They could probably run the hospice for a week on what they raised by the sale of her clothes.

It was an addiction; it was like alcoholism or drugs or gambling, and more expensive than drinking or the slot machines. Last week, when she was coming in with a bright yellow bag and an olive-green bag, Gil had caught her in the hall. Caught her. She had used the words inadvertently, without thinking, and inaccurately. For Gil was the kindest and best of men; he would never, never reproach her. The worst thing was that he would *praise* her. He would tell her it was her money, she earned more than he did anyway, she could do what she liked with it. Why shouldn't she buy herself some new clothes?

She had imagined telling him then, when they came face-to-face and she had those bags in her hands. She imagined confessing, saying to him, I've something to tell you. His face would change; he would think what everyone thought when they heard those words from their partner. She would sit on the floor at his feet—all this she imagined, building an absurd scenario—and hold his hand and tell him, I do this, I am mad, it's driving me mad, and I can't stop. I keep buying clothes. Not jewelry or ornaments or furniture or pictures, not stuff to put on my face or my hair, not even shoes or hats or gloves. I buy clothes. A dress shop is a wine bar to me. It is my casino. I can't pass it. If I go into a department store to buy a box of tissues or a bathmat, I go upstairs, I buy clothes.

He would laugh. He would be happy and relieved because she was telling him she liked buying things to wear, not that she'd met someone else and was leaving him. Kisses then and reassurances and a heartening Why shouldn't you spend your own money? He, who was so understanding, wouldn't understand this.

His voice called out, "Alison! It's ready."

They were to have a glass of wine first. This wine had been much praised on the program and he wanted her to try it. He raised his glass to her. "Do you know what today is?"

Some anniversary. It was women who were supposed to remember these things, not men. "Should I? Oh, dear."

"Not the first time we met," he said. "Not even the first time you took me out to dinner. The first time *I* took *you* out. Three years ago today."

She put into the words all the emotion with which her thoughts had charged her. "I love you."

Gil scarcely knew what clothes she possessed. He never looked in her cupboard. Sometimes, when she wore one of the new dresses or suits or shirts, he would say, "I like that. It's new, isn't it?"

"I've had it for ages. You must have seen it before." And he accepted that. He didn't notice clothes much; he wasn't interested. But when he asked, she should have told him. Or when the credit-card statements came in. Instead of paying the huge sums secretly, she should have said, "Look at this. This is what I do with my money. This is my madness, and you must stop me."

She couldn't. She was too ashamed. She even wondered what the credit-card people must think of her when month after month they assessed her expenditure and found another thousand pounds gone on clothes. The shop assistants wrote "clothes" in the space on the chit, and she had once thought, stupidly, of asking them to put "goods" instead. It was because of what she was that the humiliation was so intense, because she was clever and accomplished with a good degree and a dazzling curriculum vitae, at the top of her profession, sought after, able to ask fees that raised eyebrows but seldom deterred. And her addiction was the kind that afflicted the football pool winners or sixteen-year-old school-leavers.

They were better than she. At least they were honest and open about it. Some could be frank and admit it, even make a joke of it. A few months back she had traveled to Edinburgh with a client to make a product presentation. They had stayed overnight. Edinburgh is not a place that immediately comes to mind as a shopping center—there are many other interesting things to do there—but the client announced as soon as they got into the station taxi that she would like to spend the two hours they had to spare at the shops.

"I'm a compulsive shopper, you know. It's what gives me a buzz."

Alison had said restrainedly, "What did you want to buy?"

"Buy? Oh, I don't know. I'll know when I see it."

So Alison had gone shopping with her and seen all the signs and symptoms that she saw in herself, but with one exception: This woman was not ashamed, she was not deceitful.

"I'm crazy, really," she said when she had bought a suit she confessed she "didn't like all that much." "I've got wardrobes full of stuff I never wear." And she laughed merrily. "I suppose you plan everything you buy terribly carefully, don't you?"

And Alison, who had stood by while the suit was bought, sick with desire to buy herself, controlling herself with all her might, wearing what she now feared had been a supercilious half-smile, agreed that this was so. She smiled like a superior being, one who bought clothes when the old ones wore out.

On that trip she had managed to avoid buying anything. The energy expended in denial had left her exhausted. In London afterward she went on a dreadful splurge, like the bulimic's binge. It was that day, or the day after, she had read the piece in the paper about compulsive behavior. Eating disorders, for instance, indicated some deep-seated emotional disturbance. It was the same with gambling, even with shopping. The compulsive shopper buys as a way of masking a need for love and to cover up inadequacy.

It wasn't true. She loved Gil. She had everything she wanted. Her life was good and satisfying. The compulsion to buy had begun only when she realized she was rich, she had more than enough, she could afford it now. Only she couldn't, hardly anyone could. Hardly anyone's income could stand this drain on it.

Compulsive shopping was a cry for help. That was what the psychologists said. But help for what? For help to stop compulsive shopping?

❑   ❑   ❑

Passing the shop where she had bought the sweaters—in a taxi, for safety's sake—she reflected on something she had thought of only momentarily at the time. She had bought the sweaters without trying them on. It was as if she was saying, I don't care if they fit or not, that is not why I am buying them. I want to *buy,* not to have.

The office was in the City, in a part where there were few shops. This, of course, was a blessing, yet she had recognized lately her dissatisfaction with the absence of clothes shops, the peculiar kind of *hunger* this lack brought her. Once she was outside in the street, an almost overwhelming impulse came to get in a taxi and be taken to where the shops were. She managed to resist. She had work to do; she had to be at her desk, near those phones, beside that fax machine. But as the days passed, the shopless days, she began to think, It will be all right for me to go shopping next time I have the opportunity, it won't be sick, it won't be neurotic, because it has been so long, it has been a whole week. . . .

There was an evening when it rained and she couldn't find a taxi. Again she took the tube, and at Knightsbridge looked for a taxi to take her that half-mile. It was quite possible to walk home by residential streets, there were many options, and it was one of the most charming parts of London. Even in the rain. But compulsive shopping began before she came to the shops, she had learned that now; it was what led her steps to Sloane Street when she might so easily have taken Seville Street and Lowndes Square.

Her thoughts were strange. She recognized them as strange. Mad, perhaps. She was thinking that if she controlled herself this evening, she would not have to do so on the following day. Next day, after the client conference, she would find herself in Piccadilly, at the bottom of Bond Street, and if she walked up toward the tube station, her route would take her along Brook Street and into South Molton Street, into one of the meccas of shopping, into heaven, buying country, shopland. . . .

She passed the shop with the globular glass doorknob, and as she came to the next, already able to see ahead of her the gleam of a single shimmering garment isolated in its window, footsteps came running behind her and Gil's arm was around her, his umbrella held high over her head.

"You ought to buy that," he said. "You'd look good in that."

She shuddered. He felt the shudder and looked at her in concern.

"A designer walked over my grave," she said.

It was the time to say why she wouldn't buy the dress and

tell him why not. She couldn't do it. All she felt was resentment that he had caught up with her and, by his presence and his kind innocent suggestion, stopped her from buying it. He was like the well-intentioned friend who offers the secret drinker a double scotch.

In the morning she went in late, walking up Sloane Street. There was nothing to do before the conference. She went into the shop and bought the dress Gil had said would look good on her. She didn't try it on but told the surprised assistant it was her size, she knew it would fit. High on adrenaline, she told herself this purchase need not stop her from buying later in the day. The day was gone anyway, she thought, it was spoiled by buying the dress and there was no point in taking a stand today, a preliminary shot of the drug had gone in. If control was possible it could start tomorrow. In the office she took the dress out of her briefcase and stuffed it in a desk drawer.

The conference was over by three. For the past hour or more she had scarcely been attending. Once her own talk was over she lost interest and let her thoughts run in the direction they always did these days. Even during the talk she once or twice lost the thread of what she was saying, needed to refer to her notes, seemed to fumble with words. The company chairman asked her if she was feeling unwell. Sitting down again, taking a drink of water, she looked ahead of her to the great thoroughfare of shops waiting for her, full of things waiting to be bought, sitting there and waiting, and a huge longing took hold of her. She almost ran out of that building; she was breathless and she was thirsty, as if she had never taken a drink of that water.

On her way up Bond Street she bought a suit and a jacket. She tried both on, but it was only for form's sake and because she cringed under the shop assistant's surprised look. A taxi came as if to rescue her while she walked onward and upward, carrying her bags, but she let it pass by and turned into Brook Street. By this time, at this *stage* of her indulgence, her feet seemed to lose contact with the ground. She floated or skimmed the surface of the pavement. In the road she was always in danger of being run over. If she had met someone she knew she would have passed him by unseeing. Her body had undergone chemical changes that had a profound effect on recognition, on logical thought, on rational behavior. They negated reason. She was unable to control the urge to buy, because for these moments, this hour perhaps, she rejected a "cure"; she wanted her compulsion, she loved it, she was drunk on it.

Thoughts she had, words in her head, but they were always simple and direct. Why shouldn't I have these things? I can afford them. Why shouldn't I be well-dressed? I mustn't be guilty about this simple enjoyable *happy* pastime. . . . They repeated themselves in her mind as she floated along, aware too of her steadily beating heart.

In South Molton Street she bought a shirt and in the shop next door a skirt with a sweater that matched it. She tried neither on, and when she was outside something made her look at the label on the skirt and sweater, which showed her she had bought them two sizes too big. She stood there, in the walking street, feeling elation drop, knowing she couldn't go back in there.

She was ashamed. The fall was very swift from reckless excitement to a kind of visionary horror; it slid off her like oversize clothes slipping from her shoulders to the floor, and there came a sudden flash of appalled insight. She began to walk mechanically. Nearly at Oxford Street, she

106

put the new clothes bags into the first rubbish bin she came to. Then she put the suit and the jacket in too. She turned her back and ran.

In the taxi she was crying. The taxi driver said, "Are you okay, love?" She said she wasn't well, she would be all right in a minute. The waste, the wickedness of such waste, were what she thought of. There were thousands, millions, who never had new clothes, who wore hand-me-downs or rags or just managed to buy secondhand. She had thrown away new clothes.

For some reason she thought of Gil, who trusted and loved her. She couldn't face him again; she would have to go to some hotel for the night. By a tortuous route the taxi was winding through streets behind Broadcasting House, behind Langham Place. It came down into Regent Street and she told the driver to let her off. He didn't like that, and she gave him a five-pound note. What was five pounds? She had just thrown away two hundred times that.

Carrying only her briefcase, she went into a department store. She caught sight of herself in a mirror, her wild hair, her staring eyes, the whiteness of her face: a madwoman. Something else struck her as she paused there briefly. She wasn't well-dressed; almost any woman she passed was better-dressed than she was. Every week, nearly every day, she bought clothes, mountains of clothes, cupboardsful, clothes to be unloaded on charities or thrown away unworn, but she was dressed less well than a woman who bought what she wore out of the money a husband gave her for housekeeping.

She hated clothes. Understanding came in migrainelike flashes of light and darkness. Why had she never realized how she hated clothes? They made her feel sick, the new slightly bitter smell of them, their sinuous slithering pressures on her, surrounding her as they now did, racks of coats and jackets, suits and dresses. She was in designer country and she could smell and feel, but she saw very little. Her eyes were affected by her mental state, and a mist hung in front of them.

Fumbling, she began to slide clothes off the rack, a shirt here, a sweater there. She opened her briefcase and stuffed the things inside. A label hung out and part of a sleeve when she closed the case. She snatched a knitted garment, long and sleeveless and buttoned, and a blouse of stiff organza, another sweater, another shirt. No one saw her, or if they did, made no attempt to intervene.

She pulled a scarf from a shelf and wound it around her neck. Pulling at the ends, she thought how good it would be to lose consciousness, for the scarf quietly to strangle her. With her overflowing briefcase, too full to close, she began to walk down the stairs. No one came after her. No one had seen. On her way through leather goods she picked up a handbag, though it was unusual for her to be attracted by such things, then a wallet and a pair of gloves. She held them in one hand, while the other held the briefcase, the bigger garments over her arm.

Between the inner glass doors and the entrance doors a bell began ringing urgently. The security officer approached. She sat down on the floor with all the stolen things around her, and when he came up to her she said quite sanely, though with a break in her voice, "Help me. Someone help me."

UNACCEPTABLE LEVELS

"You shouldn't scratch it. You've made it bleed."

"It itches. It's giving me hell. You don't react to mosquito bites the way I do."

"It's just where the belt on your jeans rubs. I think I'd better put a plaster on it."

"They're in the bathroom cabinet," he said.

"I know where they are."

She removed the plaster from its plastic packing and applied it to the small of his back. He reached for his cigarettes, put one in his mouth, and lit it.

"I wonder if you're allergic to mosquito bites," she said. "I mean, I wonder if you should be taking antihistamine when you get bitten. You know, you should try one of those sprays that ease the itching."

"They don't do any good."

"How do you know if you don't try? I don't suppose smoking helps. Oh, yes, I know that sounds ridiculous to you, but smoking does affect your general health. I bet you didn't tell the doctor you had all these allergies when you were examined for that life insurance you took out."

"What do you mean, 'all these allergies'? I don't have allergies. I have rather a strong reaction to mosquito bites."

"I bet you didn't tell them you smoked," she said.

"Of course I told them. You don't mess about when you're taking out a hundred thousand pounds' worth of insurance on your life." He lit a cigarette from the stub of the last one. "Why d'you think I pay such high premiums?"

"I bet you didn't tell them you smoked forty a day."

"I said I was afraid I was a heavy smoker."

"You ought to give it up," she said. "Mind you, I'd like a thousand pounds for every time I've said that. I'd like a *pound*. You smokers don't know what it's like living with it. You don't know how you smell, your clothes, your hands, the lot. It gets in the curtains. You may laugh, but it's no joke."

"I'm going to bed," he said.

In the morning she had a shower. She made a cup of tea and brought it up to him. He stayed in bed smoking while he drank his tea. Then he had a shower.

"And wash your hair," she said. "It stinks of smoke."

He came back into the bedroom with a towel around him. "The plaster came off."

"I expect it did. I'll put another one on."

She took another plaster out of its pack.

"Did I make it bleed?"

"Of course you make it bleed when you scratch it. Here, keep still."

"You'd think it would stop itching after a couple of days, wouldn't you?"

"I told you, you should have used an antiallergenic spray. You should have taken an antihistamine. You've got a very nasty sore place there, and you're going to have to keep it covered for at least another forty-eight hours."

"Anything you say."

He lit a cigarette.

In the evening they ate their meal outdoors. It was very warm. He smoked to keep the mosquitoes away.

"Any excuse," she said.

"One of those little buggers has just bitten me in the armpit."

"Oh, for God's sake. Just don't scratch this one."

"Do you really think I should have told the insurance people I'm allergic to mosquito bites?"

"I don't suppose it matters," she said. "I mean, how could anyone tell after you were dead?"

"Thanks very much," he said.

"Oh, don't be silly. You're much more likely to die of smoking than of a mosquito bite."

Before they went to bed she renewed the plaster on his back and, because he had scratched the new one, gave him another. He could put that one on himself. He had to get up in the night; the bites drove him mad and he couldn't just lie there. He walked about the house, smoking. In the morning he told her he didn't feel well.

"I don't suppose you do if you didn't get any sleep."

"I found a packet of nicotine patches in the kitchen," he said. "Nicorella or something. I suppose that's your latest ploy to stop me smoking."

She said nothing for a moment. Then, "Are you going to give it a go, then?"

"No, thanks very much. You've wasted your moncy. D'you know what it says in the instructions? 'While using the patches it is highly dangerous to smoke.' How about that?"

"Well, of course it is."

"Why is it?"

"You could have a heart attack. It would put unacceptable levels of nicotine into your blood."

" 'Unacceptable levels'—you sound like a health minister on telly."

"The idea," she said, "is to stop smoking while using the patch. That's the point. The patch gives you enough nicotine to satisfy the craving *without* smoking."

"It wouldn't give me enough."

"No, I bet it wouldn't," she said, and she smiled.

He lit a cigarette. "I'm going to have my shower and then perhaps you'll redo those plasters for me."

"Of course I will," she said.

IN ALL HONESTY

Ever since Beatrix Cooper-Gibson had had her teeth capped she had been afraid of one or more of the crowns coming adrift while she was asleep, sticking in her throat, and choking her to death. It was in vain that her dentist told her this could never happen. Caps did loosen, it was a well-known fact, so why not hers? And why not in the night?

The result was that she became a bad sleeper. Always supposing she could get to sleep, she woke up after an hour or so and felt about in her mouth to make sure the caps were all still there. It took awhile to get to sleep again, and then she was bound to wake up after another hour and begin the exploratory process once more.

As she grew older, so her fears increased, for there were others. If she sat close to a wall she was afraid a picture might fall on her, even if she sat six inches away, a foot away, for there was no guarantee it would not fly outward in its descent. Gradually she had all the furniture moved into the center of the rooms. Flies were anathema to her, and since spiders catch flies, she allowed no spiders' webs to be removed. She was more frightened of electricity than almost anything, expected every plug to be pulled out of every socket before the household retired for the night and pulled out the plug on her bed lamp herself. This meant that if she wanted light in the night she would have to get up first to replace the plug in the socket, so she kept a flashlight on the bedside cabinet and a candle in a candlestick in case the flashlight battery failed.

Unsympathetic companions might have made her life very difficult or unhappy (or cured her of these neurotic compulsions), but Gwenda and Clive thought these anxieties only reasonable. Or Gwenda did, and Clive went along with what Gwenda thought, as she went along with what he thought, for their marriage was exceptionally harmonious. Gwenda thought Beatrix Cooper-Gibson a sensible, prudent woman.

"The house hasn't burnt down, has it?" Gwenda said. "And in all honesty"—she used this expression a lot, often when neither truth nor probity were in question—"no one's ever been hit on the head by a picture."

"And say what you like," said loyal Clive, "food poisoning has never been an issue."

These arguments had been occasioned by Beatrix Cooper-Gibson's son Alexander protesting about what he called his mother's "barminess." She was getting worse, he said. She was seventy-five, would probably live another ten years, and what further eccentricities would she develop before that?

It was in Gwenda and Clive's interest to keep Beatrix alive as long as possible. Eighty-five was nothing. Why not ninety-five, when they would be eligible for their own retirement pensions? The job was a sinecure—lovely flat, color TV and video, bathroom with Jacuzzi, personal microwave—and if Beatrix insisted that they, too, moved the furniture into the middle of each room, that was no hardship.

It signified her care and affection for them, a tenderness both returned. She didn't need much looking after, bless her, fit as a fiddle she was, wonderful for her age.

"In all honesty," Gwenda said, "it's like having one's own dear mother in one's home."

If Alexander minded that—after all, they were in Beatrix's house, not she in theirs—he gave no sign of it. He pointed out that the place had been completely rewired two years before and that his mother's dentist had assured him the cement he used to fix her caps in place would take a pulling power of five hundred horsepower to shift it.

"Accidents do happen," said Clive, a remark that earned him an encouraging smile from his wife.

Alexander cast up his eyes. His mother's latest whim was to have the whole house updated with a deep shag-pile carpet in various pale shades. She had read somewhere or heard (or invented, Alexander thought) that whereas close carpet in a dark color absorbs heat and even a certain amount of light, pale shag with inch-long fibers traps warmth and then reflects it back. It was dreadful to think, she said, of all that expensive heat being sucked up by the thin dark surface, leaving the rooms cold and probably even damp, encouraging colds, flu, bronchitis, allergies, pneumonia, catarrh, pleurisy, and hypothermia. She painted a grim picture of a dark greenish-brown tight-woven mass, fungoid or swamplike, drawing into itself, as might a carnivorous plant draw in insects, all the health-giving warmth from the central heating and radiant light from the sun.

"It will cost a bomb," said Alexander.

"So what? I'm not asking you to pay for it."

He would scarcely have minded if she had. Money was not at issue. He had as much of it as she had, and if he had made his while his father had left her hers, it was all money to be spent as money should be on an enhancement of the quality of life. But to blow it on hideous anemic floor covering, having ripped up acres of prime Wilton . . . !

"I'm going to have it done, Alexander. I can't sleep at night for worrying about it. I lie awake thinking about all that heat draining through the floors."

"Better take the doctor's sleeping pills," said Alexander.

"Oh, yes, definitely," said his mother with heavy sarcasm, "and get such a good night's sleep I choke to death on my own teeth."

The carpet fitters came in a month later and removed the chocolate and olive-green and crimson Wilton from the floors. Beatrix told them it had absorbed not only ten years of heat but also billions upon billions of microbes, and to take it away and dispose of it. The foreman took it home, had it cleaned, and relaid it all over his housing association duplex.

The shrimp-pink and albino and mouse and meal-colored shag was unrolled. Beatrix measured the strands in the pile with a ruler and found them an acceptable inch and a half long. The foreman called it four centimeters, but she wasn't having any truck with that. It took days to lay the carpet in every room of the house, Beatrix often hindering operations by reminding the workmen not to move the furniture too close to the walls and not to touch the spiders' webs.

"Oh, isn't it beautiful!" said Gwenda, clapping her hands.

"Don't you love those delicate pastel shades?"

Alexander said it wasn't exactly to his taste and his sister Julia said it would be a lot harder to keep clean.

"In all honesty," said Gwenda, "and if you don't mind me saying so, that's my problem. To be frank, I encouraged Mrs. C-G to have this lovely wall-to-wall and I'm not a bit sorry I did. Light and bright is what you need when you're young in heart if not in years."

Alexander might have said no more, for the deed was done now, and if the new carpet was more suited to high-tech or Bauhaus furniture, to walls of glass and ceilings of marble, than to his mother's early-Victorian chaise longues, family portraits, and watercolors, it was her house and her choice. But Julia was less able to contain her feelings. It was because of this failure of self-control that she came to see Beatrix less often than he did.

"I'm sorry, but I think it's totally ghastly and utterly un-suitable." Julia was a bit of a snob. "It's actually the kind of thing the working classes have in council flats." The fore-man had, and had rectified this as soon as something supe-rior was available. "I'm sorry, but it's simply not fair on this lovely old house."

Gwenda had not liked that reference to the working class, to which she belonged. She "had no time," in her own phrase, expressed only to Clive, for "Little Miss Clever." But she stood, as she always did when "the family" were all to-gether, in a submissive and perfect servantlike fashion, with her hands clasped and her head bowed. A small gentle and resigned smile tip-tilted her lips and her eyes roved apprecia-tively across the shag-pile carpet, which in this room was the color of frosted cornflakes. She did not look at Beatrix. There was no need to. She knew Beatrix was not a woman to receive criticism meekly or reproaches with a shrug.

"What did you say?" was how Beatrix began her counter-attack.

"Oh, Mama, you heard me. You know what I said."

"I know you were setting yourself up as an arbiter of taste and an expert on social distinctions." Beatrix smiled, showing off the well-anchored caps. She was not one to pull her punches. "Considering that suburban eyesore you live in with that bank clerk, I'm sure you're qualified to judge."

"Bertie is not a bank clerk. He is a departmental manager," said Julia.

"Who cares? The only thing about him that interests me is why such a boring and conventional man can't bring himself to do the traditional thing and marry you."

"You shut up, you evil-tongued old bat!"

"Excuse me," said Gwenda. "I'm intruding. I'll go, I have things to see to."

"Stay exactly where you are, Gwenda. A witness to this behavior is required. Are you going to stand there, Alexander, and let your sister speak to me like that?"

"If you don't like the way I am," said Julia, "you've only yourself to blame. You're my mother."

"Yes, indeed, and giving birth to you was the biggest mistake I ever made. The most miserable day of my life! Now, you can apologize. I never want to hear language like that again in my own drawing room. I wonder how you'll feel after I'm gone and you find I've left this 'lovely old house' to somebody else."

This was standard. Beatrix threatened to change her will every time Julia paid a visit. So far she had not done so and Julia had never apologized or changed her habit of speaking, but simply walked out of the house muttering, to return two or three months later as if nothing had happened. This time was no different, and perhaps would have had no dif-

118

ferent results if Julia had not come back with Alexander after a week had gone by.

Gwenda admitted them to the house. Letting her son have a key was not the kind of thing that suited Beatrix. The expression on Gwenda's face betrayed her feelings, astonishment at "Miss Clever's" swift return and perhaps a happy anticipation of renewed strife. Beatrix ignored her daughter. She addressed herself to Alexander, telling him of a new danger. This was from toxic rays emanating from the video recorder if tapes were used more than ten times. Ten was the crucial number. At this point chemical changes took place not in the tape itself but in the black plastic cassette that contained it and an invisible but noxious ray, or rather gas, was emitted via the medium of the television screen. She had sent Clive out to replace all the videocassettes and burn the old ones.

Alexander said it seemed very far-fetched. His sister curled back her upper lip the way people do when they smell something nasty. She said, though not referring to the poisonous videotapes, that she had been speaking about Beatrix's neuroses (her word) to a friend of hers who was a distinguished physicist. This woman had told her it was all nonsense about dark carpets absorbing heat, a complete myth.

"Women shouldn't be physicists," said Beatrix. "They should stay at home and look after the children. I blame the mess the world is in on women working."

"She hasn't got any children."

"I'm not surprised. Her reproductive processes have been poisoned by the work she does. Or pretends to do."

"To hear you talk," said Julia, "anyone would think

you'd had a dozen children instead of stopping at just the two. What happened to your reproductive processes? Or were you too selfish to have any more?"

"I'll just pop out into the kitchen and see to my casserole," said Gwenda, though making no move to go.

"Stay right where you are, please," said Beatrix. "This is it. She has done it this time. Have you ever in all your experience, Gwenda, heard a young woman utter such words to her mother?"

"Oh, leave me out of it, Mrs. C-G. I'm only a servant. I wouldn't wish to pass judgment."

"Your very tone gives you away, Gwenda. I can hear your loyalty in it. I can hear your natural deep disapproval." Beatrix had an extraordinarily loud voice for a woman of seventy-five. She raised it to its maximum decibels. "Get out of my house!"

"If I go," said Julia, "I won't come back."

"I sincerely hope not. It would give me a little holiday in my heart to have seen the last of you. I'll see *you* on Tuesday, Alexander."

And she did. But by that time she had changed her will. Gwenda brought her the mobile phone; she called Mr. Webley and asked him to lunch. He came on the Monday. Clive, who did the cooking when there was company, made *mozzarella tricolore,* chicken à la king, and charlotte russe, for both Beatrix and her solicitor were fond of their food. While they were drinking their coffee and Beatrix, but not Mr. Webley for he had to drive, was having a drambuie with it, he took his pad out of his briefcase and noted down his client's wishes: not a sausage (her words) to Julia, a token sum to Alexander, and everything else to Clive and Gwenda.

Mr. Webley remonstrated gently.

"When you've quite finished," said Beatrix, "perhaps you'll remember it's my money."

The will was drawn up and sent to Beatrix for her approval. This was not the first time this had happened, though in the past there had been different sets of beneficiaries and always the new will had been torn up or, at any rate, not returned to Mr. Webley. The old one, the one that left everything to Alexander and Julia, remained valid. But this time Beatrix had meant what she said.

She read the will carefully, and when Gwenda came into the room told her she wanted two witnesses.

"Clive and me will be happy to do that for you," said Gwenda untruthfully. She was on tenterhooks.

Beatrix gave her a long meaningful look. "That wouldn't do at all," she said. "Perhaps you'll just step across the road and ask Lady Huntly if she would be so kind as to come over for a glass of sherry. Oh, and Gwenda, if Brian is still doing the yew hedge he might come in, too. Make sure he washes his hands first."

Lady Huntly was the widow of a county councillor and Lord Lieutenant who had been knighted for giving large sums of money to the Conservative Party. She was a sprightly little old lady with bright red lips and a wig of blue curls. Sizable sums of money remained, enabling her to live in the big Edwardian turreted house opposite, keep up the BMW, and spend part of every winter in Fort Lauderdale. Her principal recreation was ballroom dancing, which she indulged in three times a week at teatime, partnered by an old man who had been her boyfriend before she met the county councillor. Beatrix liked her because she listened sympathetically to her anxieties and to some extent shared her fears about toxic videotapes and swallowing one's teeth, in Lady Huntly's case a plate.

The gardener, Brian Gospel, was a singer with a country-and-western band, his real name being Gobbett. He mowed Beatrix's lawn and trimmed her hedges between gigs. Julia said her mother should be careful and she hoped she was insured to cover all eventualities because Brian had chorea, you only had to see his tics, and was certainly unsafe around the electric trimmer. She refused to believe Beatrix when she said he was only miming an armpit guitar. He was twenty-three years old, tall, dark, and ugly in a sexy sort of way.

These were the two people Gwenda brought in to witness Beatrix's will.

"In the presence of the testatrix and of each other," said Gwenda, who had read these instructions in a pamphlet from the Citizen's Advice Bureau.

She still thought Beatrix might change her mind. She stood there with her arms folded and her head bowed, holding her breath. Beatrix signed. Lady Huntly signed, using her own Mont Blanc fountain pen. Brian signed and said he didn't suppose the ladies would fancy coming along to an evening of nostalgia and sing along with Merle Haggard's greatest hits. Fluttering her extended eyelashes, Lady Huntly said she would think about it, and after Brian had gone back to his hedge, she and Beatrix settled down to schooners of oleroso.

Jubilant in the kitchen, Gwenda said to Clive that they had done it this time. She would take the will to the post and catch the five-thirty collection.

"Or I could drive into town and drop it through Webley's letterbox."

"We don't want to do anything to draw attention to ourselves," said Gwenda. She put her arms around him, gave him a passionate kiss, and then took the will down the road, dropping it in the letterbox at ten past five.

But the next morning she wished she had let Clive do as he suggested. She had never felt so nervous. Suppose there had been a mail robbery? Such things happened. Or a wicked postman, with no idea of his duty to the post office and the public, had stolen a selection of the contents of the box in the hope of discovering five-pound notes slipped into letters? She resisted for two hours and then she phoned Mr. Webley. Mrs. Cooper-Gibson, she said, was very anxious to know if the will had arrived. Oh, yes, certainly, he had it in his hand at that moment, said Mr. Webley, sounding none too pleased and rather suspicious.

Gwenda wished she hadn't done it. What would happen if he told Beatrix? A new will? Oh, the shame and the pain! Alexander came in the afternoon and talked for a long time in a maudlin way about how much he wished his mother and sister got on better. He implied that it was largely his mother's fault. Had she thought of seeing a psychotherapist or perhaps a counselor? Beatrix told him to go, she was tired, she disliked being lectured in her own house. Coming back from virtually pushing him out of the front door, she leaned back against the wall and stamped her foot. She stamped one heavily shod, solid foot and then the other and a large oil painting in a gilt frame fell off the wall and struck her on the neck and back.

Her worst misgivings were realized. Beatrix yelled for Gwenda. She wasn't much hurt, but she was frightened. Her fears had been real and yet they had not been real; they were of the kind that wake the sufferer with vague apprehensions during the night but are not much more than an eccentricity by day, superstitious injunctions that if not obeyed may result in disaster, so why not obey them? But this had proved them right, proved *her* right. Gwenda offered to call the doctor.

"I don't want him," said Beatrix. At their last encounter she had overheard him telling Gwenda her troubles were "in the old soul's imagination."

"Well, shall I have a look at your back, Mrs. C-G?"

"No, leave me alone. Now this has happened I shan't sleep a wink. Or if I do I shall relive the nightmare of that picture falling on me."

The picture, a portrait of Beatrix's grandfather in a morning coat with some sort of chain of office hanging around his neck, was examined by Clive, who found its cord badly frayed. There must have been thirty or forty pictures of equal size and weight—if not all of such unattractive subjects—in the house, and Beatrix said she would be unable to sleep ever again until she knew all the cords had been replaced. Clive set about it straightaway, although it was half past nine in the evening.

Beatrix said, "I may be doing a very imprudent thing, Gwenda, but I am going to take a sleeping pill."

"Quite right," said Gwenda. "After all, the odds against your caps coming off and sticking in your throat must be about ten thousand to one."

"I wouldn't know about that. I'm not a bookmaker. As a matter of fact, I would normally consider the chances quite high, as you know, only not now the picture has fallen on me."

"Pardon?"

"Lightning isn't going to strike twice, is it? It's not in the nature of things for a picture to fall on me and then for my teeth to get stuck in my throat. You might as well say that tonight I'm just as much in danger as ever of being burnt to death by faulty electricity, when obviously I'm not."

"If you say so," said Gwenda doubtfully, and she found the sleeping pills and brought one to Beatrix with her hot drink.

By eleven-fifteen Clive had renewed the cords on twenty-two pictures. "I shall call it a day," he said to his wife. "Enough is enough."

"You'll check up on the electric plugs, won't you?"

Clive did. He went into his own flat and to bed just before midnight. Gwenda put her arms around him in her sleep. On the floor below, at the front of the house, in the big master bedroom newly redecorated in shell-pink shag, Beatrix lay perilously near the edge of the bed. The drug had a powerful effect on her, because in all her life she had only taken a soporific twice before. Still and totally relaxed, she lay as one dead. But some imperceptible movements must have occurred in her deep sleep, for an acute observer, if there had been one, who had watched her for the past hour would have noticed that from the center of the four-poster she had shifted in that time some six inches toward the edge. By half past midnight her gradual forward progress had increased the distance to nine inches. At one-fifteen she was poised on the very edge.

The bedclothes were not tucked in. They never were. Beatrix had another phobia about that. She insisted that an inevitable result of tucking in the bedclothes was a nightmare in which she was sewn up in a sack with a snake and a monkey and thrown in the Bosporus. So the sheet and blanket hung loose, while the quilt had slithered back to the far side of the bed. Beatrix's left arm hung over the edge. Her left leg dipped over the edge and slowly her right leg joined it. Although she was fast asleep, she waved her right arm to save herself, but nevertheless slipped forward and tumbled onto the floor.

Beatrix lay prone with her face buried in the soft long-haired pink carpet. If her progress across the bed had been backward she would have fallen into a supine position and very likely have recovered. But, still deeply asleep, she lay facedown with thick fluff pressing into her nose and mouth and it suffocated her. Within half an hour she was dead. The time was just before two.

Entering the bedroom at nine, Gwenda called out her usual merry "Good morning, Mrs. C-G," a cry that turned to a shriek of terror. Her first thought was that the most-feared had happened and Beatrix had swallowed the caps off her teeth. She told the doctor that and he reacted to what she said with suspicion, not to say indignation. By then he had seen the bruise on the back of Beatrix's neck.

The pathologist the police called in found more bruises on Beatrix's back. Gwenda was questioned. She told the detective inspector about the picture falling on Beatrix, adding that the cord holding it in place had become frayed. When no signs of fraying could be seen, Clive described how he had renewed the cord not only on the portrait of Beatrix's grandfather but on twenty-one other paintings in the house. The inspector seemed to find this very odd, especially since Alexander told him he knew nothing about a picture falling on his mother. The fear of such a thing happening was a factor in her neurosis, bearing no relation to reality.

Suspicion increased when the contents of the will were made known. The will itself was dated only two days before. Its provisions were that everything Beatrix had to leave, her house, her investments, as well as a huge capital sum, went to Clive and Gwenda. The inquest on Beatrix was adjourned while the police continued to make inquiries.

Lady Huntly told the inspector that she had been greatly surprised to be called as a witness to the will. Gwenda had rushed across the road with unseemly haste, as if it were a matter of life or death. No doubt it was. Of course, she had been able to see which way the wind was blowing as soon as she understood neither Clive nor Gwenda was to be the other witness. The inspector talked to Brian and Brian told him he had never been inside the house before and would have refused to have anything to do with this will business had not Gwenda implored him to "do this one little thing for her before the old trout changed her mind."

Mr. Webley described how astonished he had been to receive a phone call from Gwenda not five minutes after the will had come in the post. He had scarcely taken it out of its envelope. Mrs. Cooper-Gibson had often in the past talked of changing her will and the process had frequently gone as far as a draft will being drawn up or even a will itself sent to her for signature, but in these cases things had gone no further.

Julia intended to contest the will. Or she said she did. That shag carpet had been installed on Gwenda's advice, she told the inspector. Her mother would never have gotten rid of her Wilton but for Gwenda and Clive, who had gained an unhealthy hold over Beatrix. It was easy to imagine those two persuading Beatrix to break the rule of a lifetime, take a sleeping pill, and while she was unconscious roll her off the bed onto the floor and suffocate her by pressing her face into the carpet. The bruises were evidence of manhandling—what more did the police want?

Day after day Gwenda and Clive were questioned, sometimes at home, more often at the police station. They remained in Beatrix's house, *their* house now. Their flat was repeatedly searched and scrutinized, their possessions tested and photographed and surface-scraped, examined for pink fibers that might have found their way from the floor of Beatrix's bedroom into theirs. No one ever told them whether or not such fibers had been found. They had begun to be uneasy with each other, more polite and considerate than usual but with less to say.

Julia phoned or wrote letters to the police every day, quoting remarks Gwenda was alleged to have made on the state of Beatrix's health, the extent of her income, and the likelihood of her accidental death. After she had written thirty-five such letters she had a nervous breakdown, retired to a psychiatric hospital, and gave up contesting the will.

Alexander got married. He had never fancied the idea of his mother and any wife of his in conjunction.

Sometimes Clive spent the night in a cell at the police station. They were getting used to him there, put a drop of whiskey in his nighttime cocoa and gave him an extra blanket, but the law restrained them from holding him for more than twenty-four hours. Gwenda they often reduced to tears by asking her why she didn't confess and so save them all a lot of time and expense.

"We shall never give this up," said the detective inspector, "not if it takes us twenty years."

Lady Huntly refused to speak to Gwenda and Clive. She and her dancing partner ignored them pointedly, walking past with their noses in the air. All the neighbors followed suit. Mr. Webley dined out on the tale of how he had been served *mozzarella tricolore,* chicken à la king, and charlotte russe by the notorious carpet murderers.

This went on for about a year. Gwenda and Clive gave up sharing a bed. Gwenda said she couldn't sleep when the person beside her had such awful dreams, waking up with a yell two or three times in the night. Your own dreams aren't in the best of taste, Clive said, moving into the spare room.

Brian went to Nashville with the band. It was a package tour and included Graceland and Disney World, but of course they hoped to be talent-spotted. While in the United States he read a piece in a newspaper that he thought worth bringing home for the police. It told of a wealthy Texan widow from Beach City who had died through suffocation. She, too, had fallen out of bed and smothered in the shag-pile carpeting. "After a ten-month investigation," said the newspaper, "her death has been ruled due to a freak accident."

The inquest on Beatrix was reopened and a verdict of accidental death returned.

The neighbors continued to ignore Gwenda and Clive. Alexander's wife had a baby. Julia came out of hospital and wrote a long letter to Gwenda, apologizing for her insinuations and suggesting she take on, at a peppercorn rent, the flat that used to be theirs. Bertie the bank departmental manager had left her and gone to Hong Kong. Mr. Webley's partner warned him that the stories he was spreading of poisoned charlotte russe and stomach upsets after every visit he had paid to Beatrix's house might well constitute slander.

Clive and Gwenda sold the house and moved away. They also sold most of the furniture, but Clive held on to the portrait of Beatrix's grandfather in morning coat and chain of office as a keepsake. Gwenda kept the video recorder to remind her of happier days when they had been a couple, sharing their home with a woman who had been as good as a mother to them. For they were no longer together. Their marriage, for a quarter of a century so happy, had broken up.

"In all honesty," said Gwenda, for once using the phrase correctly, "did you kill her?"

"You know I didn't," said Clive. "I was asleep in bed with you. You were asleep in bed with me." He thought about that one. "Or were you?"

"You know I was, Clive."

"You were just as capable of killing her as me."

"But I didn't."

"You would say that," said Clive.

"So would you."

Clive bought a seven-room bungalow in the Isle of Wright, Gwenda a seventeenth-century farmhouse in Shropshire. Their notoriety traveled before them and they were rejected by the local inhabitants. Still, as Gwenda wrote, replying to Julia's Christmas card, there was something to be said, in all honesty, for being unhappy in luxury.

THE STRAWBERRY TREE

1 The hotel where we are staying was built by my father. Everyone assures me it is the best in Llosar and it is certainly the biggest and ugliest. From a distance it looks as if made of white cartridge paper or from hundreds of envelopes with their flaps open. Inside it is luxurious in the accepted way with sheets of bronze-colored mirrors and tiles of copper-colored marble, and in the foyer, in stone vessels of vaguely Roman appearance, stands an army of hibiscus with trumpet flowers the red of soldiers' coats.

There is a pool and a room full of machines for exercise, three restaurants, and two bars. A machine polishes your shoes and another makes ice. In the old days we used to watch the young men drink *palo* out of long thin bow-shaped vessels from which the liquor spouted in a curving stream. Now the hotel barman makes cocktails called *Mañanas* that are said to be famous. We tried them yesterday, sitting on the terrace at the back of the hotel. From there, if you are not gazing at the swimming pool as most people do, you can rest your eyes, in both senses, on the garden. There the arbutus has been planted and flourishes, its white flowers blooming and strawberry fruits ripening at the same time, something I have heard about but never seen before, for it is October and I was last here all those years ago in summer.

We have rooms with envelope balconies and a view of the bay. There are no fishing boats anymore, the pier of the old hotel with its vine canopy is gone, and the old hotel itself has become a casino. But the harbor is still there with the statue of the Virgin, *Nuestra Doña de los Marineros*, where, swimming in the deep green water, Piers and Rosario and I first saw Will sitting on the sturdy stone wall.

All along the "front," as I suppose I must call it, are hotels and restaurants, souvenir shops and tourist agencies, cafés and drinking places, where once stood a string of cottages. The church with its brown campanile and shallow pantiled roof that used to dominate this shore has been almost lost among the new buildings, dwarfed by the gigantic Thomson Holiday hotel. I asked the chambermaid if they had had jellyfish at Llosar lately, but she only shook her head and muttered about *contaminación*.

The house we were lent by José-Carlos and Micaela is still there but much "improved" and extended, painted sugar-pink and surrounded by a fence of the most elaborate wrought ironwork I have ever seen, iron lace for a giant's tablecloth around a giant's child's iced cake. I would be surprised if Rosario recognized it. Inland, things are much the same, as far as I can tell. Up to now I have not ventured there, even though we have a most efficient rented car. I climb up a little way out of the village and stare at the yellow hills, at the olive trees and junipers, and the straight wide roads that now make seams across them, but I cannot see the little haunted house, the *Casita de Golondro*. It was never possible to see it from here. A fold in the hills, crowned with woods of pine and carob, hides it. The manager of our hotel told me this morning it is now a *parador*, the first on Majorca.

When I have performed the task I came here to do I shall go and have a look at it. These state-run hotels, of which there are many on the mainland, are said to be very comfortable. We might have dinner there one evening. I shall propose it to the others. But as for removing from here to there, if any of them suggest it, I shall make up my mind to turn it down. For one thing, if I were staying there I should sooner or later have to rediscover *that* room or deliberately avoid it. The truth is I no longer want an explanation. I want to be quiet; I want, if this does not sound too ludicrous, to be happy.

My appointment in Muralla is for ten o'clock tomorrow morning with an officer of the *Guardia Civil* whose rank, I think, would correspond to our detective superintendent. He will conduct me to see what is to be seen and I shall look at the things and try to remember and give him my answer. I haven't yet made up my mind whether to let the others come with me, nor am I sure they would want to come. Probably it will be best if I do this, as I have done so much in the past, alone.

❑   ❑   ❑

2 Nearly forty years have passed since first we went to Majorca, Piers and I and our parents, to the house our Spanish cousin lent us because my mother had been ill. Her illness was depression and a general feeling of lowness and lethargy, but the cause of it was a lost child, a miscarriage. Even then, before there was real need, my parents were trying to have more children, had been trying to have more, although I was unaware of this, since soon after my own birth thirteen years before. It was as if they knew, by some sad superstitious prevision, that they would not always have their pigeon pair.

I remember the letter to my father from José-Carlos. They had fought side by side in the Spanish Civil War and been fast friends and sporadic correspondents ever since, although he was my mother's cousin, not my father's. My mother's aunt had married a Spaniard from Santander and José-Carlos was their son. Thus we all knew where Santander was but had scarcely heard of Majorca. At any rate, we had to search for it on the map. With the exception of Piers, that is. Piers would have known, Piers could have told us it was the largest of the Balearic Islands, Baleares Province in the western Mediterranean, and probably too that it covered something over fourteen hundred square miles. But one of the many many nice things about my clever brother, child of good fortune, was his modesty. Handing out pieces of gratuitous information was never his way. He too stood and looked over our father's shoulder at Goodall and Darby's *University Atlas,* a prewar edition giving pride of place to the British Empire and in which the Mediterranean was an unimportant inland sea. He looked, as we did, in silence.

The tiny Balearics floated green and gold on pale blue, held in the arms of Barcelona and Valencia. Majorca (Mallorca in brackets) a planet with attendant moons: Formentera, Cabrera, but Minorca too and Ibiza. How strange it now seems that we had never heard of Ibiza, had no idea of how to pronounce it, while Minorca was just the place a chicken was named after.

José-Carlos's house was at a place called Llosar. He described it and its setting deprecatingly, making little of the beauty, stressing rustic awkwardnesses. It was on the northwest coast, overlooking the sea, within a stone's throw of the village, but there was not much to the village, only a few little shops and the hotel. His English was so good it put us to shame, my father said. They would have to brush up their Spanish, my mother and he.

The house was ours for the months of July and August, or for us children's school holidays. We would find it very quiet, there was nothing to do but swim and lie in the sun, eat fish and drink in the local tavern, if my parents had a mind to that. In the southeast of the island were limestone caves and subterranean lakes, worth a visit if we would entrust ourselves to the kind of car we would find for hire. Tourists had begun to come, but there could not be many of these as there was only one hotel.

Llosar was marked on our map, on a northern cape of the island. The capital, Palma, looked quite big until you saw its letters were in the same size print as Alicante on the mainland. We had never been abroad, Piers and I. We were the children of war, born before it, confined by it to our own beleaguered island. And since the end of war we had been fated to wait patiently for something like this that would not cost much or demand a long-term plan.

I longed for this holiday. I had never been ill but now I dreaded some unspecified illness swooping down on me as the school term drew to its close. It was possible. Everyone, sooner or later, in those days before general immunization, had measles. I had never had it. Piers had been in hospital for an operation the previous year, but I had never so much as had my tonsils out. Anything could happen. I felt vulnerable. I lived in daily terror of the inexplicable gut pain, the rash appearing, the cough. I even began taking my temperature first thing in the morning, as my poor mother took hers, although for a different reason. They would go without me. Why not? It would be unfair to keep four people at home for the sake of one. I would be sent, after I came out of hospital, to stay with my aunt Sheila.

What happened was rather different. We were not to be a member of the party fewer but to be joined by one more. José-Carlos's second letter was even more apologetic and this time, in my view at least, with justice. He had a request. We must of course say no at once if what he asked was unacceptable. Rosario would very much like to be at the house while we were there. Rosario loved the place so much and always stayed there in the summer holidays.

"Who is he?" I said.

"He's a girl," my mother said. "José-Carlos's daughter. I should think she must be fifteen or sixteen by now."

"It's one of those Spanish names," said my father, "short for Maria of the something-or-other, Maria del Pilar, Maria del Consuelo, in this case Maria of the rosary."

I was very taken aback. I didn't want her. The idea of a Spanish girl joining us filled me with dismay. I could imagine her, big and dark, with black flowing hair and tiers of skirts that would swing as she danced, a comb and mantilla, although I stopped at the rose between her teeth.

"We can write to José-Carlos and say it's not acceptable." This seemed perfectly reasonable to me. "He says we are to, so we can. We can do it at once and she'll know in plenty of time not to be there."

My mother laughed. My father did not. Now, so long afterward, I can look back and believe he already understood the way I was and it worried him. He said gently but not smiling, "He doesn't mean it. He's being polite. It would be impossible for us to say no."

"Besides," said Piers, "she may be very nice." That was something I could never consider as possible. I was wary of almost everyone then and I have changed very little. I still prepare myself to dislike people and be disliked by them. Their uncharitableness I anticipate, their meanness and envy. When someone invites me to dinner and tells me that such-and-such an acquaintance of theirs will be there, a man or a woman I shall love to meet, I invariably refuse. I dread such encounters. The new person, in my advance estimation, will be cold, self-absorbed, malicious, determined to slight or hurt me, will be handsome or beautiful, well-dressed and brilliant, will find me unattractive or stupid, will either not want to talk to me or will want to talk with the object of causing humiliation.

I am unable to help this. I have tried. Psychotherapists have tried. It is one of the reasons why, although rich beyond most people's dreams and good-looking enough, intelligent enough and able to talk, I have led until recently a lonely life, isolated, not so much neglected as the object of remarks such as:

"Petra won't come, so there is really no point in asking her," and "You have to phone Petra or write to her so far in advance and make so many arrangements before you drop in for a cup of tea, it hardly seems worth it."

It is not so much that I am shy as that, cold myself, I understand the contempt and indifference of the cold-hearted. I do not want to be its victim. I do not want to be reduced by a glance, a laugh, a wounding comment, so that I shrivel and grow small. That is what the expression means:

137

to make someone feel small. But another phrase, when someone says he wants the earth to open and swallow him up, that I understand, that is not something I long for but something which happens to me daily. It is only in this past year that the thaw has begun, the slow delayed opening of my heart.

So the prospect of the company of Rosario spoiled for me those last days before we left for Spain. She would be nicer to look at than I was. She would be taller. Later on in life the seniority of a friend is to one's advantage, but not at thirteen. Rosario was older and therefore more sophisticated, more knowledgeable, superior and aware of it. The horrible thought had also struck me that she might not speak English. She would be a grown-up speaking Spanish with my parents and leagued with them in the great adult conspiracy against those who were still children.

So happy anticipation was spoiled by dread, as all my life it has been until now.

❑   ❑   ❑

If you go to Majorca today special flights speed you there direct from Heathrow and Gatwick and, for all I know, Stansted too. It may well be true that more people go to Majorca for their holidays than anywhere else. When we went we had to take the train to Paris and there change on to another that carried us through France and the night, passing the walls of Carcassonne at sunrise, crossing the frontier into Spain in the morning. A small, light, and probably ill-maintained aircraft took us from Barcelona to Palma and one of the hired cars, the untrustworthy rackety kind mentioned by José-Carlos, from Palma to the north.

I slept in the car, my head on my mother's shoulder, so I absorbed nothing of that countryside that was to grow so familiar to us, that was to ravish us with its beauty and in the end betray us. The sea was the first thing I saw when I woke up, of a deep, silken, peacock blue, a mirror of the bright cloudless sky. And the heat wrapped me like a shawl when I got out and stood there on dry pale stones, striped with the thin shadows of juniper trees.

I had never seen anywhere so beautiful. The shore that enclosed the bay was thickly wooded, a dark massy green, but the sand was silver. There was a skein of houses trailed along the shore, white cottages with flat pantiled roofs, the church with its clean square companile and the hotel whose terrace, hung with vines and standing in the sea, was a combination of pier and tree house. Behind all this and beyond it, behind *us* the way we had come, a countryside of yellow hills scattered with gray trees and gray stones, stretched itself out and rolled up into the mountains. And everywhere stood the cypresses like no trees I had ever seen before, blacker than holly, thin as stems, clustered like groups of pillars or isolated like single obelisks, with shadows that by evening would pattern the turf with an endlessly repeated tracery of lines. Upon all this the sun shed a dry, white, relentless heat.

Children look at things. They have nothing else to do. Later on, it is not just a matter of this life being full of care and therefore worthless if we have no time to stand and stare. We have no time, we cannot change back, that is the way it is. When we are young, before the time of study, before love, before work and a place of our own to live in, everything is done for us. If we have happy childhoods, that is, and good parents. Our meals will be made and our beds, our clothes washed and new ones bought, the means to buy earned for us, transport provided and a roof over our heads. We need not think of these things or fret about them. Time does not press its hot breath on us, saying to us, go, go, hurry, you have things to do, you will be late, come, come, hurry.

So we can stand and stare. Or lean on a wall, chin in hands, elbows on the warm rough stone, and look at what lies down there, the blue silk sea unfolding in a splash of lace on the sand, the rocks like uncut agate set in a strip of silver. We can lie in a field, without thought, only with dreams, gazing through a thousand stems of grasses at the tiny life that moves among them as between the tree trunks of a wood. In a few years' time, a very few, it will be possible no more, as all the cares of life intrude, distract the mind and spoil the day, introducing those enemies of contemplation, boredom and cold and stiffness and anxiety.

At thirteen I was at the crossing point between then and now. I could still stand and stare, dawdle and dream, time being still my toy and not yet my master, but adult worries had begun. People were real, were already the only real threat. If I wanted to stay there, leaning on my wall, from which hung like an unrolled bolt of purple velvet the climber I learned to call the bougainvillea, it was as much from dread of meeting José-Carlos and his wife Micaela and Rosario, their daughter, as from any longing for the prolongation of my beautiful view. In my mind, as I gazed at it, I was rehearsing their remarks, designed to diminish me.

"Petra!"

My father was calling me, standing outside a white house with a balcony running all the way around it at first-floor

level. Cypresses banded its walls and filled the garden behind it, like spikes of dark stalagmites. There was a girl with
him, smaller than me, I could tell even from that distance,
small and thin and with a tiny face that looked out between
great dark doors of hair, as through the opening in a gate-
way. Instead of guessing she was Rosario, I thought she must
be the child of a caretaker or cleaner. Introductions would
not be made. I scarcely glanced at her. I was already bracing
myself for the coming meeting, hardening myself, emptying
my mind. Up through the white sunlight to the house I went
and was on the step, had pushed open the front door, when
he said her name to me.

"Come and meet your cousin."

I had to turn and look then. She was not at all what I
expected. People never are and I know that—I think I even
knew it then—but this was a knowledge that made no difference. I have never been able to say, wait and see, make no
advance judgments, reserve your defense. I managed to lift
my eyes to hers. We did not shake hands but looked at each
other and said hello. She had difficulty with the H, making
it too breathy. I noticed, close up beside her, that I was an
inch taller. Her skin was pale with a glow behind it, her body
as thin as an elf's. About the hair only I had been right, and
that not entirely. Rosario's hair was the color of polished
wood, of old furniture, as smooth and shining, and about
ten times as long as mine. Later she showed me how she
could sit on it, wrap herself in it. My mother told her, but
kindly, meaning it as a compliment, that she could be Lady
Godiva in a pageant. And then, of course, Piers, who knew
the story properly, had to explain who Lady Godiva was.

Then, when we first met, we did not say much. I was too
surprised. I must say also that I was gratified, for I had ex-

pected a young lady, an amalgam of Carmen and a nun, and found instead a child with Alice in Wonderland hair and ankle socks. She wore a little short dress and on a chain around her neck a seed-pearl locket with a picture of her mother. She preceded me into the house, smiling over her shoulder in a way unmistakably intended to make me feel at home. I began to thaw and to tremble a little, as I always do. Her parents were inside with my mother and Piers, but not to stay long. Once we had been shown where to find things and where to seek help if help were needed, they were to be off to Barcelona.

We had been traveling for a day and a night and half a day. My mother went upstairs to rest in the big bed under a mosquito net. My father took a shower in the bathroom, which had no bath and where the water was not quite cold but of a delectable cool freshness.

Piers said, "Can we go in the sea?"

"If you like to." Rosario spoke the very correct, oddly accented English of one who had been taught the language with care but seldom heard it spoken by an English person. "There is no tide here. You can swim whenever you want. Shall we go now and I can show you?"

"In a place like this," said my brother, "I should like to go in the sea every day and all day. I'd never get tired of it."

"Perhaps not." She had her head on one side. "We shall see."

We did grow tired of it eventually. Or, rather, the sea was not always the sweet buoyant blessing it appeared to be that first afternoon. A plague of jellyfish came and on another day someone thought he saw a basking shark. Fishermen complained that swimmers frightened off their catch. And as a day-long occupation we grew tired of it. But that first time and for many subsequent times when we floated in its warm blue embrace and looked through depths of jade and green at the abounding marine life, at fishes and shells and the gleaming tendrils of subaqueous plants, all was perfect, all exceeded our dreams.

Our bodies and legs were white as fishes. Only our arms had a pale tan from the English summer. Piers had not been swimming since his illness, but his trunks came up just high enough to hide the scar. Rosario's southern skin was that olive color that changes only a little with the seasons, but her limbs looked brown compared to ours. We sat on the rocks in the sun and she told us we must not leave the beach without covering ourselves or walk in the village in shorts or attempt to go in the church—this one was for me—with head and arms uncovered.

"I don't suppose I shall want to go in the church," I said.

She looked at me curiously. She wasn't at all shy of us, and what we said made her laugh. "Oh, you will want to go everywhere. You will want to see everything."

"Is there much to see?" Piers was already into the way of referring back to the textual evidence. "Your father said there would only be swimming and a visit to the caves."

"The caves, yes. We must take you to the caves. There are lots and lots of things to do here, Piers."

It was the first time she had spoken his name. She pronounced it like the surname "Pearce." I saw him look at her with more friendliness, with more warmth, than before. And it is true that we are *warmed* by being called by our names. We all know people who hardly ever do it, who only do it when they absolutely must. They manage to steer conversations along, ask questions, respond, without ever using a first name. And they chill others with their apparent detachment, those others who can never understand that it is diffidence which keeps them from committing themselves to the use of names. They might get the names wrong, or use them too often, be claiming an intimacy to which they have no right, be forward, pushy, presumptuous. I know all about it, for I am one of them.

Rosario called me Petra soon after that and Piers called her Rosario. I remained, of course, on the other side of that bridge which I was not to cross for several days. We went up to the house and Rosario said,

"I'm so happy you have come."

It was not said as a matter of politeness but rapturously. I could not imagine myself uttering those words even to people I had known all my life. How could I be so forward, lay myself open to their ridicule and their sneers, *expose* myself to their scorn? Yet when they were spoken to me I felt no scorn and no desire to ridicule. Her words pleased me, they made me feel needed and liked. But that was far from understanding how to do myself what Rosario did, and forty years later I am only just learning.

"I'm so happy you have come."

She said it again, this time in the hearing of my parents.

Piers said, "We're happy to be here, Rosario."

It struck me then, as I saw him smile at her, that until then he had not really known any girls but me.

❏   ❏   ❏

3 My brother had all the gifts, looks, intellect, charm, simple niceness, and, added to these, the generosity of spirit that should come from being favored by the gods but often does not. My mother and father doted on him. They were like parents in a fairy story, poor peasants who know themselves unworthy to bring up the changeling prince some witch has put into their own child's cradle.

Not that he was unlike them, having taken for himself the best of their looks, the best features of each of them, the best of their talents, my father's mathematical bent, my mother's love of literature, the gentleness and humor of both. But these gifts were enhanced in him, he bettered them. The genes of outward appearance that met in him made for greater beauty than my mother and father had.

He was tall, taller at sixteen than my father. His hair was a very dark brown, almost black, that silky fine dark hair that goes gray sooner than any other. My father, who was not yet forty, was already gray. Piers's eyes were blue, as are all the eyes in our family except my aunt Sheila's, which are turquoise with a dark rim around the pupils. His face was not a film star's nor that of a model posing in smart clothes in an advertisement, but a Pre-Raphaelite's meticulous portrait. Have you seen Holman Hunt's strange painting of Valentine rescuing Sylvia, and the armed man's thoughtful, sensitive, gentle looks?

At school he had always been top of his class. Examinations he was allowed to take in advance of his contemporaries he always passed and passed well. He was destined to go up to Oxford at seventeen instead of eighteen. It was hard to say whether he was better at the sciences than the arts, and if it was philosophy he was to read at university, it might equally have been classical languages or physics.

Modern languages were the only subjects at which he failed to excel, at which he did no better and often less well than his contemporaries, and he was quick to point this out. That first evening at Llosar, for instance, he complimented Rosario on her English.

"How do you come to speak English so well, Rosario, when you've never been out of Spain?"

"I learn at school and I have a private teacher, too."

"We learn languages at school and some of us have private teachers, but it doesn't seem to work for us."

"Perhaps they are not good teachers."

"That's our excuse, but I wonder if it's true."

He hastened to say what a dunce he was at French, what a waste of time his two years of Spanish. Why, he would barely know how to ask her the time or the way to the village shops. She looked at him in that way she had, her head a little on one side, and said she would teach him Spanish if he liked, she would be a good teacher. No English girl ever looked at a boy like that, in a way that was frank and shrewd, yet curiously maternal, always practical, assessing the future. Her brown river of hair flowed down over her shoulders, rippled down her back, and one long tress of it lay across her throat like a trailing front of willow.

I have spoken of my brother in the past—"Piers was" and "Piers did"—as if those qualities he once had he no longer has, or as if he were dead. It is not my intention to give a false impression, but how otherwise can I recount these events? Things may be less obscure if I talk of loss rather than death, irremediable loss in spite of what has happened since, and of Piers's character only as it was at sixteen, making clear that I am aware of how vastly the personality changes in forty years, how speech patterns alter, specific learning is lost, and huge accumulations of knowledge gained. Of Piers I felt no jealousy, but I think this was a question of sex. If I may be allowed to evolve such an impossible thesis I would say that jealousy might have existed if he had been my sister. It is always possible for the sibling, the less favored, to say to herself, ah, this is the way members of the opposite sex are treated, it is different for them, it is not that I am inferior or less loved, only different. Did I say that? Perhaps, in a deeply internal way. Certain it is that the next step was never taken; I never asked, where then are the privileges that should be accorded to my difference? Where are the special favors that come the way of daughters which their brothers miss? I accepted and I was not jealous.

At first I felt no resentment that it was Piers Rosario chose for her friend and companion, not me. I observed it and told myself it was a question of age. She was nearer in age to Piers than to me. And a question too perhaps, although I had no words for it then, of precocious sex. Piers had never had a girlfriend and she, I am sure, had never had a boyfriend. I was too young to place them in a Romeo and Juliet situation, but I could see that they liked each other in the way boys and girls do when they begin to be aware of gender and the future. It did not matter because I was not excluded, I was always with them, and they were both too kind to isolate me. Besides, after a few days we found someone to make a fourth.

❑   ❑   ❑

At this time we were still enchanted, Piers and I, by the beach and all that the beach offered: miles of shore whose surface was a combination of earth and sand and from which the brown rocks sprang like living plants, a strand encroached upon by pine trees with flat umbrellalike tops and purplish trunks. The sea was almost tideless but clean still, so that where it lapped the sand there was no scum or detritus of flotsam but a thin bubbly foam that dissolved at a touch into clear blue water. And under the water lay the undisturbed marine life, the bladder weed, the green sea grass and the weedlike trees of pleated brown silk, between whose branches swam small black and silver fish, sea anemones with pulsating whiskered mouths, creatures sheathed in pink shells moving slowly across the frondy seabed.

We walked in the water, picking up treasures too numerous to carry home. With Rosario we rounded the cape to discover the other hitherto invisible side, and in places where the sand ceased, we swam. The yellow turf and the myrtle bushes and the thyme and rosemary ran right down to the sand, but where the land met the sea it erupted into dramatic rocks, the color of a snail's shell and fantastically shaped. We scaled them and penetrated the caves that pocked the cliffs, finding nothing inside but dry dust and a salty smell and, in the largest, the skull of a goat.

After three days spent like this, unwilling as yet to explore further, we made our way in the opposite direction, toward the harbor and the village where the little fishing fleet was beached. The harbor was enclosed with walls of limestone built in a horseshoe shape, and at the end of the right arm stood the statue of the Virgin, looking out to sea, her own arms held out, as if to embrace the world.

The harbor's arms rose some eight feet out of the sea,

and on the left one, opposite *Nuestra Doña,* sat a boy, his legs dangling over the wall. We were swimming, obliged to swim for the water was very deep here, the clear but marbled dark green of malachite. Above us the sky was a hot shimmering silvery-blue and the sun seemed to have a palpable touch. We swam in a wide slow circle and the boy watched us.

You could see he was not Mallorquin. He had a pale freckled face and red hair. Today, I think, I would say Will has the look of a Scotsman, the bony, earnest, clever face, the pale blue staring eyes, although in fact he was born in Bedford of London-born parents. I know him still. That is a great understatement. I should have said that he is still my friend, although the truth is I have never entirely liked him, I have always suspected him of things I find hard to put into words. Of some kind of trickery perhaps, of having deep-laid plans, of using me. Ten years ago when he caused me one of the greatest surprises of my life by asking me to marry him, I knew as soon as I had recovered it was not love that had made him ask.

In those days, in Majorca, Will was just a boy on the watch for companions of his own age. An only child, he was on holiday with his parents and he was lonely. It was Piers who spoke to him. This was typical of Piers, always friendly, warmhearted, with no shyness in him. We girls, if we had been alone, would probably have made no approaches, would have reacted to the watchful gaze of this boy on the wall by cavorting in the water, turning somersaults, perfecting our butterfly stroke and other hydrobatics. We would have *performed* for him, like young female animals under the male eye, and when the display was over have swum away.

Contingency has been called the central principle of all history. One thing leads to another. Or one thing does not lead to another because something else happens to prevent it. Perhaps, in the light of what was to come, it would have been better for all if Piers had not spoken. We would never have come to the *Casita de Golondro,* so the things that happened there would not have happened, and when we left the island to go home we would all have left. If Piers had been less than he was, a little colder, a little more reserved, more like me. If we had all been careful not to look in the boy's direction but had swum within the harbor enclosure with eyes averted, talking perhaps more loudly to each other and laughing more freely in the way people do when they want to make it plain they need no one else, another will not be welcome. Certain it is that the lives of all of us were utterly changed, then and now, because Piers, swimming close up to the wall, holding up his arm in a salute, called out,

"Hello. You're English, aren't you? Are you staying at the hotel?"

The boy nodded but said nothing. He took off his shirt and his canvas shoes. He stood up and removed his long trousers, folded up his clothes, and laid them in a pile on the wall with his shoes on top of them. His body was thin and white as a peeled twig. He wore black swimming trunks. We were all swimming around watching him. We knew he was coming in but I think we expected him to hold his nose and jump in with the maximum of splashing. Instead, he executed a perfect dive, his body passing into the water as cleanly as a knife plunged into a pool.

Of course, it was done to impress us, it was "showing off." But we didn't mind. We *were* impressed and we congratulated him. Rosario, treading water, clapped her hands.

Will had broken the ice as skillfully as his dive had split the surface of the water.

He would swim back with us, he liked "that end" of the beach.

"What about your clothes?" said Piers.

"My mother will find them and take them in." He spoke indifferently, in the tone of the spoiled only child whose parents wait on him like servants. "She makes me wear a shirt and long trousers all the time," he said, "because I burn. I turn red like a lobster. I haven't got as many skins as other people."

I was taken aback until Piers told me later that everyone has the same number of layers of skin. It is a question not of density but of pigment. Later on, when we were less devoted to the beach and began investigating the hinterland, Will often wore a hat, a big wide-brimmed affair of woven grass. He enjoyed wrapping up, the look it gave him of an old-fashioned adult. He was tall for his age, which was the same as mine, very thin and bony and long-necked.

We swam back to our beach and sat on the rocks, in the shade of a pine tree for Will's sake. He was careful, fussy even, to see that no dappling of light reached him. This, he told us, was his second visit to Llosar. His parents and he had come the previous year and he remembered seeing Rosario before. It seemed to me that when he said this he gave her a strange look, sidelong, rather intimate, mysterious, as if he knew things about her we did not. All is discovered, it implied, and retribution may or may not come. There was no foundation for this, none at all. Rosario had done nothing to feel guilty about, had no secret to be unearthed. I noticed later he did it to a lot of people and it disconcerted them. Now, after so long, I see it as a blackmailer's look, although Will as far as I know has never demanded money with menaces from anyone.

"What else do you do?" he said. "Apart from swimming?"

Nothing, we said, not yet anyway. Rosario looked defensive. After all, she almost lived here and Will's assumed sophistication was an affront to her. Had she not only three days before told us of the hundred things there were to do?

"They have bullfights sometimes," Will said. "They're in Palma on Sunday evenings. My parents went last year, but I didn't. I faint at the sight of blood. Then there are the Dragon Caves."

"*Las Cuevas del Drac,*" said Rosario.

"That's what I said, the Dragon Caves. And there are lots of other caves in the west." Will hesitated. Brooding on what possibly was forbidden or frowned on, he looked up and said in the way that even then I thought of as sly, "We could go to the haunted house."

"The haunted house?" said Piers, sounding amused. "Where's that?"

Rosario said without smiling, "He means the *Casita de Golondro.*"

"I don't know what it's called. It's on the road to Pollença—well, in the country near that road. The village people say it's haunted."

Rosario was getting cross. She was always blunt, plainspoken. It was not her way to hide even for a moment what she felt. "How do you know what they say? Do you speak Spanish? No, I thought not. You mean it is the man who has the hotel that told you. He will say anything. He told my mother he has seen a whale up close near Cabo de Pinar."

"Is it supposed to be haunted, Rosario?" said my brother.

She shrugged. "Ghosts," she said, "are not true. They don't happen. Catholics don't believe in ghosts, they're not supposed to. Father Xaviere would be very angry with me if he knew I talked about ghosts." It was unusual for Rosario to mention her religion. I saw the look of surprise on Piers's face. "Do you know it's one-thirty?" she said to Will, who had of course left his watch behind with his clothes. "You will be late for your lunch and so will we." Rosario and my brother had already begun to enjoy their particular rapport. They communicated even at this early stage of their relationship by a glance, a movement of the hand. Some sign he made, perhaps involuntary and certainly unnoticed by me, seemed to check her. She lifted her shoulders again, said, "Later on, we shall go to the village, to the lace shop. Do you like to come too?" She added, with a spark of irony, her head tilted to one side, "The sun will be going down, not to burn your poor skin that is so thin."

The lace-makers were producing an elaborate counterpane for Rosario's mother. It had occurred to her that we might like to spend half an hour watching these women at work. We walked down there at about five, calling for Will at the hotel on the way. He was sitting by himself on the terrace, under its roof of woven vine branches. Four women, one of whom we later learned was his mother, sat at the only other occupied table, playing bridge. Will was wearing a clean shirt, clean long trousers, and his grass hat, and as he came to join us he called out to his mother in a way that seemed strange to me because we had only just met, strange but oddly endearing,

"My friends are here. See you later."

Will is not like me, crippled by fear of a snub, by fear of being thought forward or pushy, but he lives in the same dread of rejection. He longs to "belong." His dream is to be a member of some inner circle, honored and loved by his fellows, privileged to share knowledge of a secret password. He once told me, in an unusual burst of confidence, that when he heard someone he knew refer to him in conversation as "my friend," tears of happiness came into his eyes.

While we were at the lace-makers' and afterward on the beach at sunset he said no more about the *Casita de Golondro,* but that night, sitting on the terrace at the back of the house, Rosario told us its story. The nights at Llosar were warm and the air was velvety. Mosquitoes there must have been, for we all had nets over our beds, but I only remember seeing one or two. I remember the quietness, the dark blue clear sky and the brilliance of the stars. The landscape could not be seen, only an outline of dark hills with here and there a tiny light glittering. The moon, that night, was increasing toward the full, was melon-shaped and melon-colored.

The others sat in deck chairs, almost the only kind of "garden furniture" anyone had in those days and which, today, you never see. I was in the hammock, a length of faded canvas suspended between one of the veranda pillars and a cypress tree. My brother was looking at Rosario in a peculiarly intense way. I think I remember such a lot about that evening because that look of his so impressed me. It was as if he had never seen a girl before. Or so I think now. I doubt if I thought about it in that way when I was thirteen. It embarrassed me then, the way he stared. She was talking about the *Casita* and he was watching her, but when she looked at him, he smiled and turned his eyes away.

Her unwillingness to talk of ghosts on religious grounds seemed to be gone. It was hard not to make the connection and conclude it had disappeared with Will's return to the hotel. "You could see the trees around the house from here," she said, "if it wasn't night," and she pointed through the darkness to the southwest where the mountains began. "*Casita* means 'little house,' but it is quite big and it is very old. At the front is a big door and at the back, I don't know what you call them, arches and pillars."

"A cloister?" said Piers.

"Yes, perhaps. Thank you. And there is a big garden with a wall around it and gates made of iron. The garden is all trees and bushes, grown over with them, and the wall is broken, so this is how I have seen the back with the word you said, the cloisters."

"But no one lives there?"

"No one has ever lived there that I know. But someone owns it, it is someone's house, though they never come. It is all locked up. Now Will is saying what the village people say, but Will *does not know* what they say. There are not ghosts, I mean there are not dead people who come back, just a bad room in the house you must not go in."

Of course, we were both excited, Piers and I, by that last phrase, made all the more enticing by being couched in English that was not quite idiomatic. But what returns to me most powerfully now are Rosario's preceding words about dead people who come back. It is a line from the past, long forgotten, which itself "came back" when some string in my memory was painfully plucked. I find myself repeating it silently, like a mantra, or like one of the prayers from that rosary for which she was named. Dead people who come back, lost people who are raised from the dead, the dead who return at last.

On that evening, as I have said, the words which followed that prophetic phrase affected us most. Piers at once asked about the "bad" room, but Rosario, in the finest tradition of tellers of ghost stories, did not admit to knowing precisely which room it was. People who talked about it said the visitor knows. The room would declare itself.

"They say that those who go into the room never come out again."

We were suitably impressed. "Do you mean they disappear, Rosario?" asked my brother.

"I don't know. I cannot tell you. People don't see them again—that is what they say."

"But it's a big house, you said. There must be a lot of rooms. If you knew which was the haunted room you could simply avoid it, couldn't you?"

Rosario laughed. I don't think she ever believed any of it or was ever afraid. "Perhaps you don't know until you are in this room and then it is too late. How do you like that?"

"Very much," said Piers. "It's wonderfully sinister. Has anyone ever disappeared?"

"The cousin of Carmela Valdez disappeared. They say he broke a window and got in because there were things to steal, he was very bad, he did no work." She sought for a suitable phrase and brought it out slightly wrong. "The black goat of the family." Rosario was justly proud of her English and only looked smug when we laughed at her. Perhaps she could already hear the admiration in Piers's laughter. "He disappeared, it is true, but only to a prison in Barcelona, I think."

156

The meaning of *golondro* she refused to tell Piers. He must look it up. That way he would be more likely to remember it. Piers went to find the dictionary he and Rosario would use and there it was: a whim, a desire.

"The little house of desire," said Piers. "You can't imagine an English house called that, can you?"

My mother came out then with supper for us and cold drinks on a tray. No more was said about the *Casita* that night and the subject was not raised again for a while. Next day Piers began his Spanish lessons with Rosario. We always stayed indoors for a few hours after lunch, siesta time, the heat being too fierce for comfort between two and four. But adolescents can't sleep in the daytime. I would wander about, fretting for the magic hour of four to come around. I read or wrote in the diary I was keeping or gazed from my bedroom window across the yellow hills with their crowns of gray olives and their embroidery of bay and juniper, like dark upright stitches on a tapestry, and now I knew of its existence, speculated about the location of the house with the sinister room in it.

Piers and Rosario took over the cool white dining room with its furnishings of dark carved wood for their daily lesson. They had imposed no embargo on others entering. Humbly, they perhaps felt that what they were doing was hardly important enough for that, and my mother would go in to sit at the desk and write a letter while Concepçion, who cleaned and cooked for us, would put silver away in one of the drawers of the press or cover the table with a clean lace cloth. I wandered in and out, listening not to Rosario's words but to her patient tone and scholarly manner. Once I saw her correct Piers's pronunciation by placing a finger on his lips. She laid on his lips the finger on which she wore a ring with two tiny turquoises in a gold setting, holding it there as if to model his mouth around the soft guttural. And I saw them close together, side by side, my brother's smooth dark head, so elegantly shaped, Rosario's crown of red-brown hair, flowing over her shoulders, a cloak of it, that always seemed to me like a cape of polished wood, with the depth and grain and gleam of wood, as if she were a nymph carved from the trunk of a tree.

So they were together every afternoon, growing closer, and when the lesson was over and we emerged all three of us into the afternoon sunshine, the beach or the village or to find Will by the hotel, they spoke to each other in Spanish, a communication from which we were excluded. She must have been a good teacher and my brother an enthusiastic pupil, for he who confessed himself bad at languages learned fast. Within a week he was chattering Spanish, although how idiomatically I never knew. He and Rosario talked and laughed in their own world, a world that was all the more delightful to my brother because he had not thought he would ever be admitted to it.

I have made it sound bad for me, but it was not so bad as that. Piers was not selfish, he was never cruel. Of all those close to me only he ever understood my shyness and my fears, the door slammed in my face, the code into whose secrets, as in a bad dream, my companions have been initiated but I have not. Half an hour of Spanish conversation and he and Rosario remembered their manners, their duty to Will and me, and we were back to the language we all had in common. Only once did Will have occasion to say,

"We all speak English, don't we?"

It was clear, though, that Piers and Rosario had begun to see Will as there for me and themselves as there for each other. They passionately wanted to see things in this way, so very soon they did. All they wanted was to be alone together. I did not know this then, I would have hated to know it. I simply could not have understood, though now I do. My brother, falling in love, into first love, behaved heroically in including myself and Will, in being polite to us and kind and thoughtful. Between thirteen and sixteen a great gulf is fixed. I knew nothing of this, but Piers did. He knew there was no bridge of understanding from the lower level to the upper, and accordingly he made his concessions.

On the day after the jellyfish came and the beach ceased to be inviting, we found ourselves deprived, if only temporarily, of the principal source of our enjoyment of Llosar. On the wall of a bridge over a dried-up river we sat and contemplated the arid but beautiful interior, the ribbon of road that traversed the island to Palma and the sidetrack that led away from it to the northern cape.

"We could go and look at the little haunted house," said Will.

He said it mischievously to "get at" Rosario, whom he liked no more than she liked him. But instead of reacting with anger or with prohibition, she only smiled and said something in Spanish to my brother.

Piers said, "Why not?"

❑   ❑   ❑

4 They were very beautiful, those jellyfish. Piers kept saying they were. I found them repulsive. Once, much later, when I saw one of the same species in a marine museum, I felt sick. My throat closed up and seemed

to stifle me, so that I had to leave. *Phylum cnidaria,* the medusa, the jellyfish. They are named for the Gorgon with her writhing snakes for hair, a glance at whose face turned men to stone.

Those that were washed up in their thousands on the shore at Llosar were of a glassy transparency the color of an aquamarine, and from their umbrella-like bodies hung crystalline feelers or stems like tassels. Or so they appeared when floating below the surface of the blue water. Cast adrift on the sand and rocks, they slumped into flat gelatinous plates, like collapsed blancmanges. My kind brother, helped by Will, tried to return them to the water, to save them from the sun, but the creeping sea, although nearly tideless, kept washing them back. It was beyond my understanding that they could bear to touch that quivering clammy jelly. Rosario, too, held herself aloof, watching their efforts with a puzzled amusement.

By the following day a great stench rose from the beach where the sun had cooked the medusas and was now hastening the process of rot and destruction. We kept away. We walked to the village and from there took the road to Pollença, which passed through apricot orchards and groves of almond trees. The apricots were drying on trays in the sun, in the heat that was heavy and unvarying from day to day. We had been in Llosar for two weeks and all that time we had never seen a cloud in the sky. Its blueness glowed with the hot light of an invisible sun. We only saw the sun when it set and dropped into the sea with a fizzle like red-hot iron plunged into water.

The road was shaded by the fruit trees and the bridge over the bed of the dried-up river, by the dense branches of pines. Here, where we rested and sat and surveyed the yellow hillsides and the olive groves, Will suggested we go to look at "the little haunted house" and my brother said, "Why not?" Rosario was smiling a small secret smile and as we began to walk on, Will and I went first and she and Piers followed behind.

It was not far to the *Casita de Golondro*. If it had been more than two kilometers, say, I doubt if even "mad tourists," as the village people called us, would have considered walking it in that heat. There was a bus that went to Palma, but it had left long before we started out. Not a car passed us and no car overtook us. It is hard to believe that in Majorca today. Of course, there were cars on the island. My parents had several times rented a car and a driver, and two days afterward we were all to be driven to the Dragon Caves. But motor transport was unusual, something to be stared at and commented upon. As we came to the side road that would lead to the *Casita*, an unmetaled track, a car did pass us, an aged Citroën, its black bodywork much scarred and splintered by rocks, but that was the only one we saw that day.

The little haunted house, the little house of a whim, of desire, was scarcely visible from this road. A dense concentrated growth of trees concealed it. This wood, composed of trees unknown to us, carob and holm oak and witches' pines, could be seen from Llosar, a dark opaque blot on the bleached yellows and grays, while the house could not. Even here the house could only be glimpsed between tree trunks, a segment of wall in faded ocherish plaster, a shallow roof of pantiles. The plastered wall that surrounded the land that Piers called the "demesne" was too high for any of us to see over, and our first sight of the *Casita* was through the broken bars and loops and curlicues of a pair of padlocked wrought-iron gates.

We began to follow the wall along its course, which soon left the road and climbed down the hillside among rocky outcroppings and stunted olive trees, herb bushes and myrtles, and in many places split open by a juniper pushing aside in its vigorous growth stones and mortar. If we had noticed the biggest of these fissures from the road we might have saved ourselves half a kilometer's walking. Only Rosario objected as Will began to climb through. She said something about our all being too old for this sort of thing, but my brother's smile—she saw it too—told us how much this amused him. It was outside my understanding then, but not now. You see, it was very unlike Piers to enter into an adventure of this kind. He really would have considered himself too old and too responsible as well. He would have said a gentle "no" and firmly refused to discuss the venture again. But he had agreed and he had said, "Why not?" I believe it was because he saw the *Casita* as a place where he could be alone with Rosario.

Oh, not for a sexual purpose, for making love, that is not what I mean. He would not, surely, at that time, at that stage of their relationship, have thought in those terms. But only think, as things were, what few opportunities he had even to talk to her without others being there. Even their afternoon Spanish lessons were subject to constant interruption. Wherever they went I, or Will and I, went with them. On the veranda, in the evenings, I was with them. It would not have occurred to me not to be with them and would have caused me bitter hurt, as my brother knew, if the most tactful hint was dropped that I might leave them on their own. I think it must be faced, too, that my parents would not at all have liked the idea of their being left alone together, would have resisted this vigorously even perhaps to the point of taking us home to England.

Had he talked about this with Rosario? I don't know. The fact is that she was no longer opposed to taking a look at the "little haunted house" while formerly she had been very positively against it. If Piers was in love with her she was at least as much in love with him. From a distance of forty years I am interpreting words and exchanged glances, eyes meeting and rapturous looks, for what they were, the signs of first love. To me then they meant nothing unless it was that Piers and Rosario shared some specific knowledge connected with the Spanish language that gave them a bond from which I was shut out.

The garden was no longer much more than a walled-off area of the hillside. It was irredeemably overgrown. Inside the wall a few trees grew of a kind not to be seen outside. Broken stonework lay about among the myrtles and arbutus, the remains of a fountain and moss-grown statuary. The air was scented with bay, which did not grow very profusely elsewhere, and there were rosy pink heathers in flower as tall as small trees. Paths there had once been, but these were almost lost under the carpet of small tough evergreens. In places it was a battle to get through, to push a passage between thorns and bay and laurels, but our persistence brought us through the last thicket of juniper into a clearing paved in broken stone. From there the house could suddenly be seen, alarmingly close to us, its cloisters only yards away. It was like being in a dream where distance means very little and miles are crossed in an instant. The house appeared, became visible, as if it had stepped out to meet us.

It was not a "little" house. This is a relative term and the people who named it may have owned a palace somewhere else. To me it seemed a mansion, bigger than any house I had ever been in. José-Carlos's villa in Llosar and our house in London could have both been put inside the *Casita* and lost somewhere among its rooms.

Its surface was plastered and the plaster in many places had fallen away, exposing pale brickwork beneath. The cloisters were composed of eight arches supported on pillars Will said were "Moorish," though without, I am sure, quite knowing what this meant. Above was a row of windows, all with their shutters open, all with stone balconies, a pantiled overhang, another strip of plaster, carved or parged in panels, and above that the nearly flat roof of pink tiles.

Within the cloister, on the left-hand side of a central door, was (presumably) the window that Carmela Valdez's cousin had broken. Someone had covered it with a piece of canvas nailed to the frame, plastic not being in plentiful supply in those days. Will was the first of us to approach nearer to the house. He was wearing his grass hat and a long-sleeved shirt and trousers. He picked at the canvas around the broken window until a corner came away, and peered in.

"There's nothing inside," he said. "Just an old empty room. Perhaps it's *the* room."

"It's not." Rosario offered no explanation as to how she knew this.

"I could go in and open the door for you."

"If it's *the* room you won't come out again," I said.

"There's a table in there with a candle on it." Will had his head inside the window frame. "Someone's been eating and they've left some bread and stuff behind. What a stink, d'you reckon it's rats?"

"I think we should go home now." Rosario looked up into Piers's face and Piers said very quickly,

"We won't go in now, not this time. Perhaps we won't ever go in."

Will withdrew his head and his hat fell off. "I'm jolly well going in sometime. I'm not going home without getting in there. We go back home next week. If we go now I vote we all come back tomorrow and go in there and explore it and then we'll *know*."

He did not specify exactly what it was we should know, but we understood him. The house was a challenge to be accepted. Besides, we had come too far to be daunted now. And yet it remains a mystery to me today that we, who had the beaches and the sea, the countryside, the village, the boats that would take us to Pinar or Formentor whenever we wished to go, were so attracted by that deserted house and its empty rooms. For Piers and Rosario perhaps it was a trysting place, but what was there about it so inviting, so enticing, to Will and me?

Will himself expressed it, in words used by many an explorer and mountaineer. "It's *there*."

On the following day we all went to the *Cuevas del Drac*. Will's parents, whom our parents had got to know, came too and we went in two cars. Along the roadside between C'an Picafort and Arta grew the arbutus that Will's mother said would bear white flowers and red fruit simultaneously in a month or two. I wanted to see that, I wondered if I ever would. She said the fruit was like strawberries growing on branches.

"They look like strawberries but they have no taste."

That is one of the few remarks of Iris Harvey's I can remember. Remember word for word, that is. It seemed sad to me then, but now I see it as an aphorism. The fruit of the arbutus is beautiful, red and shiny; it looks like strawberries but it has no taste.

The arbutus grew only in this part of the island, she said. She seemed to know all about it. What she did not know was that these same bushes grew in profusion around the little haunted house. I identified them from those on the road to C'an Picafort, from the smooth glossy leaves that were like the foliage of garden shrubs, not wild ones. Among the broken stones, between the junipers and myrtle, where all seemed dust-dry, I had seen their leaves, growing as green as if watered daily.

On our return we inspected the beach and found the jellyfish almost gone, all that remained of them gleaming patches on the rocks like snails' trails. Piers and Rosario sat on the veranda doing their Spanish and Will went back to the hotel, his shirt cuffs buttoned, his hat pulled well down.

"Tomorrow then," Piers had said to him as he left, and Will nodded.

That was all that was necessary. We did not discuss it among ourselves. A decision had been reached, by each of us separately and perhaps simultaneously, in the cars or the caves or by the waters of the subterranean lake. Tomorrow we should go into the little haunted house, to see what it was like, because it was *there*. But a terrible or wonderful thing happened first. It was terrible or wonderful, depending on how you looked at it, how *I* looked at it, and I was never quite sure how that was. It filled my mind; I could scarcely think of anything else.

My parents had gone to bed. I was in the bedroom I

shared with Rosario, not in bed but occupied with arranging my mosquito net. This hotel where we now are is air-conditioned, you never open the windows. You move and dress and sleep in a coolness that would not be tolerated in England, a breezy chill that is very much at odds with what you can see beyond the glass, cloudless skies and a desiccated hillside. I liked things better when the shutters could be folded back against the walls, the casements opened wide, and the net in place so that you were protected from insects, yet in an airy room. The net hung rather like curtains do from a tester on an English four-poster and that morning, in a hurry to be off to the *Cuevas,* I had forgotten to close them.

Having made sure there were no mosquitoes inside the curtains, I drew them and switched off the light so that no more should be attracted into the room. Sentimentally, rather than kill it, I carried a spider in my handkerchief to the window to release it into the night. The moon was waxing, a pearl drop, and the stars were brilliant. While dark, with a rich clear somehow shining darkness, everything in the little walled garden could clearly be seen. All that was missing was not clarity but color. It was a monochrome world out there, black and silver and pewter and pearl and lead-color and the opaque velvety grayness of stone. The moon glowed opal-white and the stars were not worlds but light-filled holes in the heavens.

I did not see them at first. I was looking past the garden at the spread of hills and the mountains beyond, serrated ranges of darkness against the pale shining sky, when a faint sound or tiny movement nearer at hand drew my eyes downward. They had been sitting together on the stone seat in the deep shade by the wall. Piers got up and then Rosario did. He was much taller than she, he was looking down at her and she up at him, eye to eye. He put his arms around her and his mouth on hers and for a moment, before they stepped back into the secretive shadow, they seemed to me so close that they were one person, they were like two cypresses intertwined and growing as a single trunk. And the shadow they cast was the long spear shape of a single cypress on moon-whitened stone.

I was very frightened. I was shocked. My world had changed in a moment. Somewhere, I was left behind. I turned away with the shocked rejecting movement of someone who has seen a violent act. Once inside my mosquito net, I drew its folds about me and lay hidden in there in the dark. I lay there rigid, holding my hands clasped, then turned onto my face with my eyes crushed into the pillow.

Rosario came upstairs and into our room and spoke softly to me, but I made her no answer. She closed the door and I knew she was undressing in the dark. In all my life I had never felt so lonely. I would never have anyone, I would always be alone. Desertion presented itself to me as a terrible reality to be confronted, not to be avoided, and the last image that was before me when sleep came was of getting up in the morning and finding them all gone, my parents and Piers and Rosario, the hotel empty, the village abandoned, Majorca a desert island and I its only wild, lost, crazed inhabitant. Not quite the last image. That was of the twin-trunked cypress tree in the garden, its branches interwoven and its shadow a single shaft.

❑   ❑   ❑

5 We entered the little house of desire, the little haunted house *(la casita que tiene fantasmas)* by the front door, Rosario going first. Will had climbed in through the broken window and opened the door inside the cloisters. It had the usual sort of lock that can be opened by turning a knob on the inside but from the outside only with a key. Piers followed her and I followed him, feeling myself to be last, the least there, the unwanted.

This, of course, was not true. The change was in my mind, not in outward reality. When I got up that morning it was not to find myself deserted, abandoned in an alien place by all those close to me, but treated exactly as usual. Piers was as warm to me as ever, as *brotherly,* my parents as affectionate, Rosario the same kind and interested companion. I was different. I had seen and I was changed.

As I have said, I could think of nothing else. What I had seen did not excite or intrigue me, nor did I wish not to have seen it, but rather that it had never happened. I might have been embarrassed in their company, but I was not. All I felt, without reason, was that they liked each other better than they liked me, that they expressed this in a way neither of them could ever have expressed it to me, and that, obscurely but because of it, *because of something he did not and could not know,* Will too must now prefer each of them to me.

On the way to the *Casita* I had said very little. Of course, I expected Piers to ask me what was the matter. I would have told him a lie. That was not the point. The point was that I was unable to understand. Why, why? What made them do that, behave in the way I had seen them in the garden? Why had they spoiled things? For me, they had become different people. They were strangers. I saw them as mysterious beings. It was my first glimpse of the degree to which human

169

beings are unknowable, my first intimation of what it is that makes for loneliness. But what I realized at the time was that we who had been a cohesive group were now divided into two parts: Piers and Rosario, Will and me.

Yet I had not chosen Will. We *choose* very few of the people we know and call our friends. In various ways they have been thrust upon us. We never have the chance to review a hundred paraded before us and out of them choose one or two. I knew nothing of this then and I resented Will for being Will, cocky, intrusive, with his red hair and his thin vulnerable skin, his silly hat, and for being so much less nice to know than either my brother or Rosario. But he was for me and they were not, not anymore. I sensed that he felt much the same way about me. I was the third best but all he could get, his companion by default. This was to be my future lot in life—and perhaps his, but I cared very little about that. It was because of this, all this, that as we entered the *Casita,* Piers and Rosario going off into one of the rooms, Will making for the hall at the front of the house, I left them and went up the staircase on my own.

I was not afraid of the house, at least not then. I was too sore for that. All my misery and fear derived from human agency, not the supernatural. If I thought of the "bad room" at all, it was with that recklessness, that fatalism, which comes with certain kinds of unhappiness: things are so bad that *anything* which happens will be a relief—disaster, loss, death. So I climbed the stairs and explored the house, looking into all the rooms, without trepidation and without much interest.

It was three stories high. With the exception of a few objects difficult to move or detach, heavy mirrors on the walls in gilded frames, an enormous bed with black oak headboard and bedposts, a painted wooden press, it was not furnished. I heard my brother's and Rosario's voices on the staircase below and I knew somehow that Piers would not have remained in the house and would not have let us remain if there had been furniture and carpets and pictures there. He was law-abiding and responsible. He would not have trespassed in a place he saw as someone's home.

But this house had been deserted for years. Or so it seemed to me. The mirrors were clouded and blue with dust. The sun bore down unchecked by shutters or curtains and its beams were layers of sluggishly moving dust that stretched through spaces of nearly intolerable heat. I suppose it was because I was a child from a northern country that I associated hauntings with cold. Although everything I had experienced since coming to Llosar taught otherwise, I had expected the *Casita de Golondro* to be cold inside and dark.

The heat was stifling and the air was like a gas. What you breathed was a suspension of warm dust. The windows were large and hazy dusty sunshine filled the house; it was nearly as light as outside. I went to the window in one of the rooms on the first floor, meaning to throw it open, but it was bolted and the fastenings too stiff for me to move. It was there, while I was struggling with the catch, that Will crept up behind me and when he was only a foot away made that noise children particularly associate with ghosts, a kind of warbling crescendo, a howling siren-sound.

"Oh, shut up," I said. "Did you think I couldn't hear you? You made more noise than a herd of elephants."

He was undaunted. He was never daunted. "Do you know the shortest ghost story in the world? There was this man reached out in the dark for a box of matches but before he found them they were stuck into his hand."

I pushed past him and went up the last flight of stairs. Piers and Rosario were nowhere to be seen or heard. I saw the double cypress tree again and its shadow and felt sick. Somewhere they were perhaps doing that again now, held close together, looking into each other's eyes. I stood in the topmost hallway of the house, a voice inside me telling me what it has often told me since, when human relations are in question: don't think of them, forget them, stand alone, you are safer alone. But my brother . . . ? It was different with my brother.

The rooms on the top floor had lower ceilings, were smaller than those below and even hotter. It sounds incomprehensible if I say that these attics were like cellars, but so it was. They were high up in the house, high under the roof, but they induced the claustrophobia of basements, and there seemed to be weighing on them a great pressure of tiers of bricks and mortar and tiles.

What happened to me next I feel strange about writing down. This is not because I ever doubted the reality of the experience or that time has dimmed it but really because, of course, people don't believe me. Those I have told—a very few—suggest that I was afraid, expectant of horrors, and that my mind did the rest. But I was *not* afraid. I was so unafraid that even Will's creeping up on me had not made me jump. I was expectant of nothing. My mind was full of dread, but it was dread of rejection, of loneliness, of others one by one discovering the secret of life and I being left in ignorance. It was fear of losing Piers.

All the doors to all the rooms had been open. In these circumstances, if you then come upon a closed door, however miserable you may be, however distracted, natural

172

human curiosity will impel you to open it. The closed door was at the end of the passage on the left. I walked down the passage, through the stuffiness, the air so palpable you almost had to push it aside, tried the handle, opened the door. I walked into a rather small oblong room with, on its left-hand wall, one of those mirrors, only this one was not large or gilt-framed or fly-spotted, but rather like a window with a plain wooden frame and a kind of shelf at the bottom of it. I saw that it was a mirror but I did not look into it. Some inner voice was warning me not to look into it.

The room was dark. No, not dark, but darker than the other rooms. Here, although apparently nowhere else, the shutters were closed. I took a few steps into the warm gloom and the door closed behind me. Hindsight tells me that there was nothing supernatural or even odd about this. It had been closed while all the others in the house were open, which indicates that it was a "slamming" door or one which would only remain open when held by a doorstop. I did not think of this then. I thought of nothing reasonable or practical, for I was beginning to be frightened. My fear would have been less if I could have let light in, but the shutters, of course, were on the outside of the window. I have said it was like a cellar up there. I felt as if I was in a vault.

Something held me there as securely as if I were chained. It was as if I had been tied up preparatory to being carried away. And I was aware that behind me, or rather to the left of me, was that mirror into which I must not look. Whatever happened I must not look into it and yet something impelled me to do so; I *longed* to do so.

How long did I stand there, gasping for breath, in that hot timeless silence? Probably for no more than a minute or two. I was not quite still, for I found myself very gradually rotating, like a spinning top that is slowing before it dips and falls on its side. Because of the mirror I closed my eyes. As I have said, it was silent, with the deepest silence I have ever known, but the silence was broken. From somewhere, or inside me, I heard my brother's voice.

I heard Piers say, "Where's Petra?"

When I asked him about this later he denied having called me. He was adamant that he had not called. Did I imagine his voice just as I then imagined what I saw? Very clearly I heard his voice call me, the tone casual. But concerned, for all that, caring.

"Where's Petra?"

It broke the invisible chains. My eyes opened onto the hot, dusty, empty room. I spun around with one hand out, reaching for the door. In doing so I faced the mirror, I moved through an arc in front of the mirror, and saw, not myself, *but what was inside it.*

Remember that it was dark. I was looking into a kind of swimming gloom and in it the room was reflected but in a changed state, with two windows where no windows were, and instead of myself the figure of a man in the farthest corner pressed up against the wall. I stared at him, the shape or shade of a bearded ragged man, not clearly visible but clouded by the dark mist that hung between him and me. I had seen that bearded face somewhere before—or only in a bad dream? He looked back at me, a look of great anger and malevolence. We stared at each other and as he moved away from the wall in my direction, I had a momentary terror he would somehow break through the mirror and be upon me. But as I flinched away, holding up my hands, he opened the reflected door and disappeared.

I cried out then. No one had opened the door on my side of the mirror. It was still shut. I opened it, came out and stood there, my back to the door, leaning against it. The main passage was empty and so was the side passage leading away to the right. I ran along the passage, feeling I must not look back, but once around the corner at the head of the stairs I slowed and began walking. I walked down, breathing deeply, turned at the foot of the first flight, and began to descend the second. There I met Piers coming up.

What I would best have liked was to throw myself into his arms. Instead, I stopped and stood above him, looking at him.

"Did you call me?" I said.

"No. When do you mean? Just now?"

"A minute ago."

He shook his head. "You look as if you've seen a ghost."

"Do I?" Why didn't I tell him? Why did I keep silent? Oh, I have asked myself enough times. I have asked myself why that warning inner voice did not urge me to tell and so, perhaps, save him. No doubt I was afraid of ridicule, for even then I never trusted to kindness, not even to his. "I went into a room," I said, "and the door closed on me. I was a bit scared, I suppose. Where are the others?"

"Will found the haunted room. Well, he says it's the haunted room. He pretended he couldn't get out."

How like Will that was! There was no chance for me now, even if I could have brought myself to describe what had happened. My eyes met Piers's eyes and he smiled at me reassuringly. Never since in all my life have I so longed to take someone's hand and hold it as I longed then to take my brother's. But all that was possible for me was to grip my own left hand in my right and so hold everything inside me.

We went down and found the others and left the house. Will pinned the canvas back over the broken window and we made our way home in the heat of the day. The others noticed I was unusually quiet and they said so. There was my chance to tell them, but of course I could not. Will had stolen a march on me. But there was one curious benefit deriving from what had happened to me in the room with the closed shutters and the slamming door. My jealousy, resentment, insecurity I suppose we would call it now, over Piers and Rosario had quite gone. The new anxiety had cast the other out.

Nothing would have got me back to the *Casita*. As we walked across the hillside, among the prickly juniper and the yellow broom, the green-leaved arbutus and the sage, I was cold in the hot sun; I was staring ahead of me, afraid to look back. I did not look back once. And later that day, gazing across the countryside from my bedroom window, although the *Casita* was not visible from there, I would not even look in its direction, I would not even look at the ridge of hillside that hid it.

❑   ❑   ❑

That evening Piers and Rosario went out alone together for the first time. There was no intention to deceive, I am sure, but my parents thought they had gone with me and Will and Will's mother to see the country dancing at Muro. It was said the *ximbombes* would be played, and we wanted to hear them. Piers and Rosario had also shown some interest in these Mallorquin drums, but they had not come with us.

Will thought they had gone with my parents to see the Roman theater, newly excavated at Puerto de Belver, although by then it was too dark to see anything.

When we got home they were already back. They were out on the veranda, sitting at the table. The moon was bright and the cicadas very noisy and of course it was warm, the air soft and scented. I had not been alone at all since my experience of the morning and I did not want to be alone then, shrouded by my mosquito net and with the moonlight making strange patterns on the walls. But almost as soon as I arrived home Rosario got up and came upstairs to bed. We hardly spoke; we had nothing to say to each other anymore.

Next evening they went out together again. My father said to Piers,

"Where are you going?"

"For a walk."

I thought he would say, "Take Petra," because that was what he was almost certain to say, but he did not. His eyes met my mother's. Did they? Can I remember that? I am sure their eyes must have met and their lips twitched in small indulgent smiles.

It was moonlight. I went upstairs and looked out of the window of my parents' room. The village was a string of lights stretched along the shore, a necklace in which, here and there, beads were missing. The moon did not penetrate these dark spaces. A thin phosphorescence lay on the calm sea. There was no one to be seen. Piers and Rosario must have gone the other way, into the country behind. I thought, Suppose I turn around and there, in the corner of this room, in the shadows, that man is.

I turned quickly and of course there was nothing. I ran downstairs and to while away the evening, my parents and I, we played a lonely game of beggar-my-neighbor. Piers and Rosario walked in at nine. On the following day we were on the beach where Will, for whom every day was April Fool's Day, struck dismay into our hearts with a tale of a new invasion of jellyfish. He had seen them heading this way from the hotel pier.

This was soon disproved. Will was forgiven because it was his next but last day. He boasted a lot about what he called his experiences in the "haunted room" of the *Casita* two days before, claiming that he had had to fight with the spirits who tried to drag him through the wall. I said nothing; I could not have talked about it. When siesta time came I lay down on my bed and I must have slept, for Rosario had been on the other bed but was gone when I awoke, although I had not heard or seen her leave.

They were gone, she and my brother, when I came downstairs, and the rest of us were preparing to go with Will and his parents in a hired car to see the gardens of a Moorish estate.

"Piers and Rosario won't be coming with us," my mother said, looking none too pleased, and feeling perhaps that politeness to the Harveys demanded more explanation. "They've found some local fisherboy to take them out in his boat. They said, would you please excuse them."

Whether this fisherboy story was true or not, I don't know. I suspect my mother invented it. She could scarcely say—well, not in those days—"My son wants to be alone with his girlfriend." Perhaps there was a boy and a boat and perhaps this boy was questioned when the time came. I expect everyone who might have seen or spoken to Piers and

Rosario was questioned, everyone who might have an idea of their whereabouts, because they never came back.

❑   ❑   ❑

6 In those days there were few eating places on the island, just the dining rooms of the big hotels or small local *tabernas*. On our way back from the Moorish gardens we found a restaurant, newly opened with the increase of tourism, at a place called Petra. Of course, this occasioned many kindly jokes on my name and the proprietor of the *Restorán del Toro* was all smiles and welcome.

Piers and Rosario's evening meal was to have been prepared by Concepçion. She was gone when we returned and they were still out. My parents were cross. They were abstracted and unwilling to say much in front of me, although I did catch one sentence, an odd one and at the time incomprehensible.

"Their combined ages only add up to thirty-one!"

It is not unusual to see displeasure succeeded by anxiety. It happens all the time. *They're late, it's inexcusable, where are they, they're not coming, something's happened.* At about half past nine this changeover began. I was questioned. Did I have any idea where they might be going? Had they said anything to me?

We had no telephone. That was far from unusual in a place like that forty years ago. But what use could we have put it to if we had had one? My father went out of the house and I followed him. He stood there looking up and down the long shoreline. We do this when we are anxious about people who have not come, whose return is delayed, even

179

though if they are there, hastening toward us, we only shorten our anxiety by a moment or two. They were not there. No one was there. Lights were on in the houses and the strings of colored lamps interwoven with the vine above the hotel pier, but no people were to be seen. The waning moon shone on an empty beach where the tide crawled up a little way and trickled back.

Apart from Concepçion, the only people we really knew were Will's parents, and when another hour had gone by and Piers and Rosario were not back my father said he would walk down to the hotel, there to consult with the Harveys. Besides, the hotel had a phone. It no longer seemed absurd to talk of phoning the police. But my father was making a determined effort to stay cheerful. As he left, he said he was sure he would meet Piers and Rosario on his way.

No one suggested I should go to bed. My father came back, not with Will's parents, who were phoning the police "to be on the safe side," but with Concepçion, at whose cottage in the village he had called. Only my mother could speak to her, but even she could scarcely cope with the Mallorquin dialect. But we soon all understood, for in times of trouble language is transcended. Concepçion had not seen my brother and cousin that evening and they had not come for the meal she prepared for them. They had been missing since five.

That night remains very clearly in my memory, every hour distinguished by some event. The arrival of the police, the searching of the beach, the assemblage in the hotel foyer, the phone calls that were made from the hotel to other hotels, notably the one at Formentor, and the incredible inefficiency of the telephone system. The moon was only just past the full and shining it seemed to me for longer than usual, bathing the village and shoreline with a searching whiteness, a providential floodlighting. I must have slept at some point, we all must have, but I remember the night as white and wakeful. I remember the dawn coming with tuneless birdsong and a cool pearly light.

The worst fears of the night gave place in the warm morning to what seemed like more realistic theories. At midnight they had been dead, drowned, but by noon theirs had become a voluntary flight. Questioned, I said nothing about the cypress tree, entwined in the garden, but Will was not so reticent. His last day on the island had become the most exciting of all. He had seen Piers and Rosario kissing, he said, he had seen them holding hands. Rolling his eyes, making a face, he said they were "in lo-ove." It only took a little persuasion to extract from him an account of our visit to the *Casita* and a quotation from Piers, probably Will's own invention, to the effect that he and Rosario would go there to be alone.

The *Casita* was searched. There was no sign that Piers and Rosario had been there. No fisherman of Llosar had taken them out in his boat, or no one admitted to doing so. The last person to see them, at five o'clock, was the priest who knew Rosario and who had spoken to her as they passed. For all that, there was for a time a firm belief that my brother and Rosario had run away together. Briefly, my parents ceased to be afraid and their anger returned. For a day or two they were angry, and with a son whose behavior had scarcely ever before inspired anger. He who was perfect had done this most imperfect thing.

Ronald and Iris Harvey postponed their departure. I think Iris liked my mother constantly telling her what a rock she was and how we could not have done without her. José-

Carlos and Micaela were sent for. As far as I know they uttered no word of reproach to my parents. Of course, as far as I know is not very far. And I had my own grief—no, not that yet. My wonder, my disbelief, my panic.

Piers's passport was not missing. Rosario was in her own country and needed no passport. They had only the clothes they were wearing. Piers had no money, although Rosario did. They could have gone to the mainland of Spain. Before the hunt was up they had plenty of time to get to Palma and there take a boat for Barcelona. But the police found no evidence to show that they had been on the bus that left Llosar at six in the evening, and no absolute evidence that they had not. Apart from the bus the only transport available to them was a hired car. No one had driven them to Palma or anywhere else.

The difficulty with the running away theory was that it did not at all accord with their characters. Why would Piers have run away? He was happy. He loved school, he had been looking forward to this sixth form year, then to Oxford. My mother said, when Will's mother presented to her yet again the "Romeo and Juliet" theory,

"But we wouldn't have stopped him seeing his cousin. We'd have invited her to stay. They could have seen each other every holiday. We're not strict with our children, Iris. If they were really that fond of each other, they could have been engaged in a few years. But they're so young!"

At the end of the week a body was washed up on the beach at Alcudia. It was male and young, had a knife wound in the chest, and for a few hours was believed to be that of Piers. Later that same day a woman from Muralla identified it as a man from Barcelona who had come at the beginning of the summer and been living rough on the beach. But that stab wound was very ominous. It alerted us all to terrible ideas.

The *Casita* was searched again and its garden. A rumor had it that part of the garden was dug up. People began remembering tragedies from the distant past, a suicide pact in some remote inland village, a murder in Palma, a fishing boat disaster, a mysterious unexplained death in a hotel room. We sat at home and waited, and the time our departure from the island was due came and went. We waited for news, we three with José-Carlos and Micaela, all of us but my mother expecting to be told of death. My mother, then and in the future, never wavered in her belief that Piers was alive and soon to get in touch with her.

After a week the Harveys went home, but not to disappear from our lives. Iris Harvey had become my mother's friend, they were to remain friends until my mother's death, and because of this I continued to know Will. He was never very congenial to me; I remember to this day the *enjoyment* he took in my brother's disappearance, his unholy glee and excitement when the police came, when he was permitted to be with the police on one of their searches. But he was in my life, fixed there, and I could not shed him. I never have been able to do so.

One day, about three weeks after Piers and Rosario were lost, my father said,

"I am going to make arrangements for us to go home on Friday."

"Piers will expect us to be here," said my mother. "Piers will write to us here."

My father took her hand. "He knows where we live."

"I shall never see my daughter again," Micaela said.

"We shall never see them again, you know that, we all know

it, they're dead and gone." And she began crying for the first time, the unpracticed sobs of the grown-up who has been tearless for years of happy life.

My father returned to Majorca after two weeks at home. He stayed in Palma and wrote to us every day, the telephone being so unreliable. When he wasn't with the police he was traveling about the island in a rented car with an interpreter he had found, making inquiries in all the villages. My mother expected a letter by every post, not from him but from Piers. I have since learned that it is very common for the mothers of men who have disappeared to refuse to accept that they are dead. It happens all the time in war when death is almost certain but cannot be proved. My mother always insisted Piers was alive somewhere and prevented by circumstances from coming back or from writing. What circumstances these could possibly have been she never said, and arguing with her was useless.

The stranger thing was that my father, who in those first days seemed to accept Piers's death, later came part of the way around to her opinion. At least, he said it would be wrong to talk of Piers as dead, it would be wrong to give up hope and the search. That was why, during the years ahead, he spent so much time, sometimes alone and sometimes with my mother, in the Balearics and on the mainland of Spain.

Most tragically, in spite of their brave belief that Piers would return or the belief that they *voiced*, they persisted in their determination to have more children, to compensate presumably for their loss. At first my mother said nothing of this to me and it came as a shock when I overheard her talking about it to Iris Harvey. When I was fifteen she had a miscarriage and later that year, another. Soon after that she began to pour out to me her hopes and fears. I cannot have known then that my parents were doomed to failure, but I seemed to know, I seemed to sense in my gloomy way perhaps, that something so much wished-for would never happen. It would not be allowed by the fates who rule us.

"I shouldn't be talking like this to you," she said, and perhaps she was right. But she went on talking like that. "They say that longing and longing for a baby prevents you having one. The more you want it the less likely it is."

This sounded reasonable to me. It accorded with what I knew of life.

"But no one tells you how to stop longing for something you long for," she said.

When they went to Spain I remained behind. I stayed with my aunt Sheila, who told me again and again she thought it a shame my parents could not be satisfied with the child they had. I should have felt happier in her house if she had not asked quite so often why my mother and father did not take me with them.

"I don't want to go back there," I said. "I'll never go back."

❑　❑　❑

7 The loss of his son made my father rich. His wealth was the direct result of Piers's disappearance. If Piers had come back that night we should have continued as we were, an ordinary middle-class family living in a semide-tached suburban house, the breadwinner a surveyor with the local authority. But Piers's disappearance made us rich and at the same time did much to spoil Spain's Mediterranean coast and the resorts of Majorca.

He became a property developer. José-Carlos, already in the building business, went into partnership with him, raised the original capital, and as the demands of tourism increased, they began to build. They built hotels: towers and skyscrapers, shoebox shapes and horseshoe shapes, hotels like ziggurats and hotels like Piranesi palaces. They built holiday flats and plazas and shopping precincts. My father's reason for going to Spain was to find his son; his reason for staying was this new enormously successful building enterprise.

He built a house for himself and my mother on the northwest coast at Puerto de Soller. True to my resolve, I never went there with them, and eventually my father bought me a house in Hampstead. He and my mother passed most of their time at Puerto de Soller, still apparently trying to increase their family, even though my mother was in her mid-forties, still advertising regularly for Piers to come back to them, wherever he might be. They advertised, as they had done for years, in the *Majorca Daily Bulletin* as well as Spanish national newspapers and the *Times*. José-Carlos and Micaela, on the other hand, had from the first given Rosario up as dead. My mother told me they never spoke of her. Once, when a new acquaintance asked Micaela if she had any children, she had replied with a simple no.

If they had explanations for the disappearance of Piers and Rosario, I never heard them. Nor was I ever told what view was taken by the National Guard, severe brisk-spoken men in berets and brown uniforms. I evolved theories of my own. They *had* been taken out in a boat, had both drowned, and the boatman been too afraid later to admit his part in the affair. The man whose body was found had killed them, hidden the bodies and then killed himself. My parents were right up to a point and they had run away together, being afraid of even a temporary enforced separation, but before they could get in touch had been killed in a road accident.

"That's exactly when you would know," Will said. "If they'd died in an accident that's when it would have come out."

He was on a visit to us with his mother during the school summer holidays, a time when my parents were always in England. The mystery of my brother's disappearance was a subject of unending interest to him. He never understood, and perhaps that kind of understanding was foreign to his nature, that speculating about Piers brought me pain. I remember to this day the insensitive terms he used. "Of course they've been bumped off," was a favorite with him, and "They'll never be found now, they'll just be bones by now."

But equally he would advance fantastic theories of their continued existence. "Rosario had a lot of money. They could have gone to Spain and stopped in a hotel and stolen two passports. They could have stolen passports from the other guests. I expect they earned money singing and dancing in cafés. Spanish people like that sort of thing. Or she could have been someone's maid. Or an artist's model. You can make a lot of money at that. You sit in a room with all your clothes off and people who're learning to be artists sit around and draw you."

Tricks and practical jokes still made a great appeal to him. To stop him making a phone call to my mother and claiming to be, with the appropriate accent, a Frenchman who knew Piers's whereabouts, I had to enlist the help of his own mother. Then, for quite a long time, we saw nothing of Ronald and Iris Harvey or Will in London, although I believe they all went out to Puerto Soller for a holiday. Will's reappearance in my life was heralded by the letter of condolence he wrote to me seven years later when my mother died.

He insisted then on visiting me, on taking me about, and paying a curious kind of court to me. Of my father he said, with his amazing insensitivity,

"I don't suppose he'll last long. They were very wrapped up in each other, weren't they? He'd be all right if he married again."

My father never married again and, fulfilling Will's prediction, lived only another five years. Will did not marry either, and I always supposed him homosexual. My own marriage to the English partner in the international corporation begun by my father and José-Carlos took place three years after my mother's death. Roger was very nearly a millionaire by then, two and a half times my age. We led the life of rich people who have too little to do with their time, who have no particular interests and hardly know what to do with their money.

It was not a happy marriage. At least I think not; I have no idea what other marriages are like. We were bored by each other and frightened of other people, but we seldom expressed our feelings and spent our time traveling between our three homes and collecting seventeenth-century furniture. Apart from platitudes, I remember particularly one thing Roger said to me:

"I can't be a father to you, Petra, or a brother."

By then my father was dead. As a direct result of Piers's death I inherited everything. If he had lived or there had been others, things would have been different. Once I said to Roger,

"I'd give it all to have Piers back."

As soon as I had spoken I was aghast at having expressed my feelings so freely, at such a profligate flood of emotion. It was so unlike me. I blushed deeply, looking fearfully at Roger for signs of dismay, but he only shrugged and turned away. It made things worse between us. From that time I began talking compulsively about how my life would have been changed if my brother had lived.

"You would have been poor," Roger said. "You'd never have met me. But I suppose that might have been preferable."

That sort of remark I made often enough myself. I took no notice of it. It means nothing but that the speaker has a low self-image and no one's could be lower than mine, not even Roger's.

"If Piers had lived my parents wouldn't have rejected me. They wouldn't have made me feel that the wrong one of us died, that if I'd died they'd have been quite satisfied with the one that was left. They wouldn't have wanted more children."

"Conjecture," said Roger. "You can't know."

"With Piers behind me I'd have found out how to make friends."

"He wouldn't have been behind you. He'd have been off. Men don't spend their lives looking after their sisters."

When Piers and Rosario's disappearance was twenty years in the past a man was arrested in the South of France and charged with the murder, in the countryside between

Bedarieux and Lodeve, of two tourists on a camping holiday. In court it was suggested that he was a serial killer and over the past two decades had possibly killed as many as ten people, some of them in Spain, one in Ibiza. An insane bias against tourists was the motive. According to the English papers, he had a violent xenophobia directed against a certain kind of foreign visitor.

This brought to mind the young man's body with the stab wound that had been washed up on the beach at Alcudia. And yet I refused to admit to myself that this might be the explanation for the disappearance of Piers and Rosario. Like my parents, Roger said, I clung to a belief, half fantasy, half hope, that somewhere they were still alive. It was a change of heart for me, this belief, it came with my father's death, as if I inherited it from him along with all his property.

And what of the haunted house, the *Casita de Golondro?* What of my strange experience there? I never forgot it, I even told Roger about it once, to have my story received with incomprehension and the remark that I must have been eating some indigestible Spanish food. But in the last year of his life we were looking for a house to buy, the doctors having told him he should not pass another winter in a cold climate. Roger hated "abroad," so it had to be in England, Cornwall, or the Channel Islands. In fact no house was ever bought, for he died that September, but in the meantime I had been viewing many possibilities and one of these was in the south of Cornwall, near Falmouth.

It was a Victorian house and big, nearly as big as the *Casita,* ugly Gothic but with wonderful views. An estate agent took me over it and, as it turned out, I was glad of his company. I had never seen such a thing before, or thought I had not, an internal room without windows. Not uncommon, the young man said, in houses of this age, and he hinted at bad design.

This room was on the first floor. It had no windows but the room adjoining it had, and in the wall that separated the two was a large window with a fanlight in it that could be opened. Thus light would be assured in the windowless room, if not much air. The Victorians distrusted air, the young man explained.

I looked at this dividing window and twenty-eight years fell away. I was thirteen again and in the only darkened room of a haunted house, looking into a mirror. But now I understood. It was not a mirror. It had not been reflecting the room in which I stood but affording me a sight of a room beyond, a room with windows and another door, and of its occupant. For a moment, standing there, remembering that door being opened, not a reflected but a real door, I made the identification between the man I had seen, the man at the wheel of the battered Citroën, and the serial killer of Bedarieux. But it was too much for me to take, I was unable to handle something so monstrous and so ugly. I shuddered, suddenly seeing impenetrable darkness before me, and the young man asked me if I was cold.

"It's the house," I said. "I wouldn't dream of buying a house like this."

Will was staying with us at the time of Roger's death. He often was. In a curious way, when he first met Roger, before we were married, he managed to present himself in the guise of my rejected lover, the devoted admirer who knows it is all hopeless but who cannot keep away, so humble and selfless is his passion. Remarks such as "may the best man win" and "some men have all the luck" were sometimes uttered by him, and this from someone who had never so much as touched my hand or spoken to me a word of affection. I explained to Roger, but he thought I was being modest. What other explanation could there be for Will's devotion? Why else but from long-standing love of me would he phone two or three times a week, bombard me with letters, angle for invitations? Poor Roger had made his fortune too late in life to understand that the motive for pursuing me might be money.

Roger died of a heart attack sitting at his desk in the study. And there Will found him when he went in with an obsequious cup of tea on a tray, even though we had a housekeeper to do all that. He broke the news to me with the same glitter-eyed relish as when I remembered him recounting to the police tales of the little haunted house. His voice was lugubrious but his eyes full of pleasure.

Three months later he asked me to marry him. Without hesitating for a moment, I refused.

"You're going to be very lonely in the years to come."

"I know," I said.

❑   ❑   ❑

8 Never once did I seriously think of throwing in my lot with Will. But that was a different matter from telling him I had no wish to see him again. He was distasteful to me with his pink face, the color of raw veal, the ginger hair that clashed with it, and the pale blue bird's-egg eyes. His heart was as cold as mine but hard in a way mine never was. I disliked everything about him, his insensitivity, the pleasure he took in cruel words. But for all that, he was my friend, he was my only friend. He was a man to be taken about by. If he hinted to other people that we were lovers, I neither confirmed nor denied it. I was indifferent. Will pleaded poverty so often since he had been made redundant by his company that I began allowing him an income, but instead of turning him into a remittance man, this only drew him closer to me.

I never confided in him, I never told him anything. Our conversation was of the most banal. When he phoned—I *never* phoned him—the usual platitudes would be exchanged and then, desperate, I would find myself falling back on that well-used silence-filler and ask him,

"What have you been doing since we last spoke?"

When I was out of London, at the house in Somerset or the "castle," a castellated shooting lodge Roger had bought on a whim in Scotland, Will would still phone me but would reverse the charges. Sometimes I said no when the operator asked me if I would pay for the call, but Will—thick-skinned mentally, whatever his physical state might be—simply made another attempt half an hour later.

It was seldom that more than three days passed without our speaking. He would tell me about the shopping he had done, for he enjoys buying things, troubles with his car, the failure of the electrician to come, the cold he had had, but never of what he might understand love to be, of his dreams or his hopes, his fear of growing old and of death, not even what he had been reading or listening to or looking at. And I was glad of it, for I was not interested and I told him none of these things either. We were best friends with no more intimacy than acquaintances.

The income I allowed him was adequate, no more, and he was always complaining about the state of his finances. If I had to name one topic we could be sure of discussing whenever we met or talked, it would be money. Will grumbled about the cost of living, services bills, fares, the small amount of tax he had to pay on his pension and what he got from me, the price of food and drink and the cost of the upkeep of his house. Although he did nothing for me, a fiction was maintained that he was my personal assistant, "secretary" having been rejected by him as beneath the dignity of someone with his status and curriculum vitae. Will knew very well that he had no claim at all to payment for services rendered, but for all that he talked about his "salary," usually to complain that it was pitifully small. Having arrived—without notice—to spend two weeks with me in Somerset, he announced that it was time he had a company car.

"You've got a car," I said.

"Yes," he said, "a rich man's car."

What was that supposed to mean?

"You need to be rich to keep the old banger on the road," he said, as usual doubling up with mirth at his own wit.

But he nagged me about that car in the days to come. What was I going to do with my money? What was I saving it for, I who had no child? If he were in my place it would give him immense pleasure to see the happiness he could bring to others without even noticing the loss himself. In the end I told him he could have my car. Instead of my giving it in part exchange for a new one, he could have it. It was a rather marvelous car, only two years old and its sole driver had been a prudent middle-aged woman, that favorite of insurers, but it was not good enough for Will. He took it but he complained, and we quarreled. I told him to get out, and he left for London in my car.

Because of this I said nothing to him when the lawyer's

letter came. We seldom spoke of personal things, but I would have told him about the letter if we had been on our normal terms. I had no one else to tell and he, anyway, was the obvious person. But for once, for the first time in all those years, we were out of touch. He had not even phoned. The last words he had spoken to me, in hangdog fashion, sidling out of the front door, were a truculent muttered plea that in spite of everything I would not stop his allowance.

So the letter was for my eyes only, its contents for my heart only. It was from a firm of solicitors in the City and was couched in gentle terms. Nothing, of course, could have lessened the shock of it, but I was grateful for the gradual lead-up, and for such words as "claim," "suggest," "allege," and "possibility." There was a softness, like a tender touch, in being requested to prepare myself and told that at this stage there was no need at all for me to rush to certain conclusions.

I could not rest but paced up and down, the letter in my hand. Then, after some time had passed, I began to think of hoaxes; I remembered how Will had wanted to phone my mother and give her that message of hope in a Frenchman's voice. Was this Will again? It was the solicitors I phoned, not Will, and they told me, yes, it was true that a man and a woman had presented themselves at their offices, claiming to be Mr. and Mrs. Piers Sunderton.

❑   ❑   ❑

9 I am not a gullible person. I am cautious, unfriendly, morose, and antisocial. Long before I became rich I was suspicious. I distrusted people and questioned their motives, for nothing had ever happened to me to make me believe in disinterested love. All my life I had never been loved, but the effect of this was not to harden me but to keep me in a state of dreaming of a love I had no idea how to look for. My years alone have been dogged by a morbid fear that everyone who seems to want to know me is after my money.

There were in my London house a good many photographs of Piers. My mother had cherished them religiously, although I had hardly looked at them since her death. I spread them out and studied them: Piers as a baby in my mother's arms, Piers as a small child, a schoolboy, with me, with our parents and me. Rosario's coloring I could remember, her sallow skin and long hair, the rich brown color of it, her smallness of stature and slightness, but not what she looked like. That is, I had forgotten her features, their shape, arrangement, and juxtaposition. Of her I had no photograph.

From the first, even though I had the strongest doubts about this couple's identity as my brother and his wife, I never doubted that any wife he might have had would be Rosario. Illogical? Absurd? Of course. Those convictions we have in the land of emotion we can neither help nor escape from. But I told myself as I prepared for my taxi ride to London Wall that if it was Piers that I was about to see, the woman with him would be Rosario.

I was afraid. Nothing like this had happened before. Nothing had *got this far* before. Not one of the innumerable "sightings" in those first months, in Rome, in Naples, Madrid, London, the Tyrol, Malta, had resulted in more than the occasional deprecating phone call to my father from whatever police force it might happen to be. Later on there had been claimants, poor things who presented themselves at my door and who lacked the sense even to learn the most elementary facts of Piers's childhood, fair-haired men, fat men, short men, men too young or too old. There were probably ten of them. Not one got farther than the hall. But this time I was afraid, this time my intuition spoke to me, saying, "He has come back from the dead," and I tried to silence it, I cited reason and caution, but again the voice whispered, and this time more insistently.

They could be changed out of all knowledge. What was the use of looking at photographs? What use are photographs of a boy of sixteen in recognizing a man of fifty-six? I waited in an anteroom for three minutes. I counted those minutes. No, I counted the seconds that composed them. When the girl came back and led me in, I was trembling.

The solicitor sat behind a desk and on a chair to his left and a chair to his right sat a tall thin gray man and a small plump woman, very Spanish-looking, her face brown and still smooth, her dark hair sprinkled with white pulled severely back. They looked at me and the two men got up. I had nothing to say, but the tears came into my eyes. Not from love or recognition or happiness or pain but for time that does such things to golden lads and girls, which spoils their bodies and ruins their faces and lays dust on their hair.

My brother said, "Petra," and my sister-in-law, in that voice I now remembered so precisely, in that identical heavily accented English, "Please forgive us, we are so sorry."

I wanted to kiss my brother, but I could hardly go up to a strange man and kiss him. My tongue was paralyzed. The lawyer began to talk to us, but of what he said I have no recollection; I took in none of it. There were papers for me to see, so-called "proofs," but although I glanced at them, the print was invisible. Speech was impossible, but I could think. I was thinking, I will go to my house in the country, I will take them with me to the country.

Piers had begun explaining. I heard something about Madrid and the South of France, I heard the word "ashamed" and the words "too late," which someone has said are the saddest in the English language, and then I found a voice in which to say,

"I don't need to hear that now, I understand, you can tell me all that later, much later."

The lawyer, looking embarrassed, muttered about the "inevitable ensuing legal proceedings."

"What legal proceedings?" I said.

"When Mr. Sunderton has satisfied the court as to his identity, he will naturally have claim on your late father's property."

I turned my back on him, for I knew Piers's identity. Proofs would not be necessary. Piers was looking down, a tired, worn-out man, a man who looked unwell. He said, "Rosario and I will go back to our hotel now. It's best for us to leave it to Petra to say when she wants another meeting."

"It's best," I said, "for us to get to know each other again. I want you both to come to the country with me."

We went, or rather Rosario and I went, to my house near Wincanton. Piers was rushed to hospital almost before he set foot over my threshold. He had been ill for weeks, had appendicitis that became peritonitis, and they operated on him just in time.

Rosario and I went to visit him every day. We sat by his bedside and we talked; we all had so much to say. And I was fascinated by them, by this middle-aged couple who had once like all of us been young but who nevertheless seemed to have passed from adolescence into their fifties without the intervention of youth and middle years. They had great tenderness for each other. They were perfectly suited. Rosario seemed to know exactly what Piers would want, that he only liked grapes that were seedless, that although a reader he would only read magazines in hospital, that the slippers he required to go to the dayroom must be of the felt, not the leather, kind. He disliked chocolates; it was useless bringing any.

"He used to love them," I said.

"People change, Petra."

"In many ways they don't change at all."

I questioned her. Now that the first shock and joy were passed I could not help assuming the role of interrogator, I could not help putting their claim to the test, even though I knew the truth so well. She came through my examination very well. Her memory of Majorca in those distant days was even better than mine. I had forgotten—although I recalled it when she reminded me—our visit to the monastery at Lluc and the sweet voices of the boy choristers. Our parents' insistence that while in Palma we all visited the *Mansion de Arte*, this I now remembered, and the Goya etchings bored us but my mother made us all look at.

José-Carlos and Micaela had both been dead for several years. I could tell she was unhappy speaking of them; she seemed ashamed. This brought us to the stumbling block, the difficulty that reared up every time we spoke of their disappearance. Why had they never got in touch? Why had they allowed us all, in such grief, to believe them dead?

She—and later Piers—could give me no reason except their shame. They could not face my parents and hers; it was better for us all to accept that they were dead. To explain why they had run away in the first place was much easier.

"We pictured what they would all say if we said we were in love. Imagine it! We were sixteen and fifteen, Petra. But we were right, weren't we? You could say we're still in love, so we were right."

"They wouldn't have believed you," I said.

"They would have separated us. Perhaps they would have let us meet in our school holidays. It would have killed us, we were dying for each other. We couldn't live out of sight of the other. That feeling has changed now, of course it has. I am not dying, am I, though Piers is in the hospital and I am here? It wasn't just me, Petra, it was Piers too. It was Piers's idea for us to—go."

"Did he think of his education? He was so brilliant, he had everything before him. To throw it up for—well, he couldn't tell it would last, could he?"

"I must tell you something, Petra. Piers was not so brilliant as you thought. Your father had to see Piers's headmaster just before you came on that holiday. He was told Piers wasn't keeping up with his early promise, he wouldn't get that place at Oxford, the way he was doing he would be lucky to get to a university at all. They kept it a secret. You weren't told, even your mother wasn't, but Piers knew. What had he to lose by running away with me?"

"Well, comfort," I said, "and his home and security and me and his parents."

"He said—forgive me—that I made up for all that."

She was sweet to me. Nothing was too much trouble for her. I, who had spent so much time alone that my tongue was stiff from disuse, my manners reclusive, now found myself caught up in her gaiety and her charm. She was the first person I have ever known to announce in the morning *ideas* for how to spend the day, even if those notions were often only that I should stay in bed while she brought me my breakfast and then that we should walk in the garden and have a picnic lunch there. When there was a need for silence, she was silent, and when I longed to talk but scarcely knew how to begin she would talk to me, soon involving us in a conversation of deep interest and a slow realization of the tastes we had in common. Soon we were companions, and by the time Piers came home, friends.

Until we were all together again I had put off the discussion of what happened on the day they ran away. Each time Rosario had tried to tell me I silenced her and asked for more about how they had lived when first they came to the Spanish mainland. Their life at that time had been a series of adventures, some terrible, some hilarious. Rosario had a gift for storytelling and entertained me with her tales while we sat in the firelight. Sometimes it was like one of those old Spanish picaresque novels, full of event, anecdote, strange characters, and hairsbreadth escapes, not all of it I am afraid strictly honest and aboveboard. Piers had changed very quickly, or she had changed him.

They had worked in hotels, their English being useful. Rosario had even been a chambermaid. Later they had been guides, and at one time, in a career curiously resembling Will's scenario, had sung in cafés to Piers's hastily improvised guitar-playing. In her capacity as a hotel servant—they were in Madrid by this time—Rosario had stolen two passports from guests and with these they had left Spain and traveled about the South of France. The names of the passport holders became their names, and in them they were married at Nice when he was eighteen and she seventeen.

"We had a little boy," she said. "He died of meningitis

when he was three and after that no more came."

I thought of my mother and put my arms around her. I, who have led a frozen life, have no difficulty in showing my feelings to Rosario. I, in whom emotion has been something to shrink from, can allow it to flow freely in her company and now in my brother's. When he was home again, well now and showing in his face some vestiges of the Piers I had known so long ago, I found it came quite naturally to go up to him, take his hand and kiss his cheek. In the past I had noticed, while staying in other people's houses, the charming habit some have of kissing their guests good night before everyone retires to their rooms. For some reason, a front of coldness perhaps, I had never been the recipient of such kisses myself. But now—and amazing though it was, I made the first move myself—I was kissing both of them good night and we exchanged morning kisses when we met next day.

One evening, quite late, I asked them to tell me about the day itself, the day that ended so terribly in fear and bright empty moonlight. They looked away from me and at each other, exchanging a rueful nostalgic glance. It was Rosario who began the account of it.

It was true that they had met several times since that first time in the little haunted house. They could be alone there without fear of interruption and there they had planned, always fearfully and daringly, their escape. I mentioned the man I had seen, for now I was sure it had been a man seen through glass and no ghost in a mirror, but it meant nothing to them. At the *Casita* they had always found absolute solitude. They chose that particular day because we were all away at the gardens but made no other special preparations, merely boarding the afternoon bus for Palma a little way outside the village. Rosario, as we had always known, had money. She had enough to buy tickets for them on the boat from Palma to Barcelona.

"If we had told them or left a note they would have found us and brought us back," Rosario said simply.

She had had a gold chain around her neck with a cameo that they could sell, and a gold ring on her finger.

"The ring with the two little turquoises," I said.

"That was the one. I had it from my grandmother when I was small."

They had sold everything of value they had, Piers's watch and his fountain pen and his camera. The ring saved their lives, Piers said, when they were without work and starving. Later on they became quite rich, for Piers, like my father, used tourism to help him, went into partnership with a man they met in a café in Marseille, and for years they had their own hotel.

There was only one question left to ask. Why did they ever come back?

They had sold the business. They had read in the deaths column of a Spanish newspaper they sometimes saw that Micaela, the last of our parents, was dead. Apparently, the degree of shame they felt was less in respect to me. I could understand that, I was only a sister. Now I think I understood everything. Now when I looked at them both, with a regard that increased every day, I wondered how I could ever have doubted their identities, how I could have seen them as old, as unutterably changed.

The time had come to tell Will. We were on speaking terms again. I had mended the rift myself, phoning him for the first time ever. It was because I was happy and happiness made me kind. During the months Piers and Rosario had been with me he had phoned as he always did, once or twice we had met away from home, but I had not mentioned them. I did not now, I simply invited him to stay.

To me they were my brother and sister-in-law, familiar loved figures with faces already inexpressibly dear, but he I knew would not know them. I was not subjecting them to a test, I needed no test, but the idea of their confronting each other without preparation amused me. A small deception had to be practiced and I made them reluctantly agree to my introducing them as "my friends Mr. and Mrs. Page."

For a few minutes he seemed to accept it. I watched him; I noticed his hands were trembling. He could bear his suspicion no longer and burst out:

"It's Piers and Rosario, I know it is!"

The years could not disguise them for him, although they each separately confessed to me afterward that if they had not been told they would never have recognized him. The red-headed boy with "one skin too few" was not just subsumed in the fat red-faced bald man but utterly lost.

Whether their thoughts often returned to those remarks the solicitor had made on the subject of legal proceedings I cannot say. When mine did for the second time I spoke out. We were too close already for litigation to be conceivable. I told Piers that I would simply divide all my property in two, half for them and half for me. They were shocked, they refused, of course they did. But eventually I persuaded them. What was harder for me to voice was my wish that the property itself should be divided in two, the London house, the Somerset farm, my New York apartment, literally split down the middle. Few people had ever wanted much of my company in the past, and I was afraid they would see this as a bribe or as taking advantage of my position of power. But all Rosario said was,

204

"Not too strictly down the middle, Petra, I hope. It would be nicer to *share.*"

All I stipulated was that in my altered will I should leave all I possessed to my godchild and cousin, Aunt Sheila's daughter, and Piers readily agreed, for he intended to leave everything he had to the daughter of his old partner in the hotel business.

So we lived. So we have lived for rather more than a year now. I have never been so happy. Usually it is not easy to make a third with a married couple. Either they are so close that you are made to feel an intruder or else the wife will see you as an ally to side with her against her husband. And when you are young the danger is that you and the husband will grow closer than you should. With Piers and Rosario things were different. I truly believe that each wanted my company as much as they wanted each other's. In those few months they came to love me and I, who have loved no one since Piers went away, reciprocated. They have shown me that it is possible to grow warm and kind, to learn laughter and pleasure, after a lifetime of coldness. They have unlocked something in me and liberated a lively spirit that must always have been there but that languished for long years, chained in a darkened room.

❑   ❑   ❑

It is two weeks now since the Majorcan police got in touch with me and told me what the archaeologists had found. It would be helpful to them and surely of some satisfaction to myself to go to Majorca and see what identification I could make, not of remains, it was too late for that, but of certain artifacts found in the caves.

We were in Somerset and once more Will was staying with us. I suggested we might all go. All those years I had avoided revisiting the island, but things were different now. Nothing I could see there could cause me pain. While I had Piers and Rosario I was beyond pain; it was as if I was protected inside the warm shell of their affection.

"In that case," Will said, "I don't see the point of going. You know the truth. These bits of jewelry, clothes, whatever they are, can't be Piers's and Rosario's because they sold theirs, so why try to identify what in fact you can't identify?"

"I want to see the place again," I said. "I want to see how it's changed. This police thing, that's just an excuse for going there."

"I suppose there will be bones too," he said, "and maybe more than bones even after so long." He has always had a fondness for the macabre. "Did the police tell you how it all got into the caves?"

"Through a kind of pothole from above, they think, a fissure in the cliff top that was covered by a stone."

"How will you feel about going back, Piers?" asked Rosario.

"I shan't know till I get there," he said, "but if Petra goes we go too. Isn't that the way it's always going to be?"

❑   ❑   ❑

10 When I woke up this morning it was with no sense of impending doom. I was neither afraid nor hopeful. I was indifferent. This was no more than a chore I must perform for the satisfaction of officials, as a "good citizen." For all that, I found my room confining in spite of the wide-open windows, the balcony and view of the sea, and canceling my room-service order, I went down to breakfast.

To my surprise I found the others already there in the terrace dining room. It was not quite warm enough to sit outside so early. They were all unaware of my approach, were talking with heads bent and close together above the table. I was tempted to come up to them in silence and lay a light loving hand on Rosario's shoulder, but somehow I knew that this would make her start. Instead I called out a "good morning" that sounded carefree because it was.

Three worried faces were turned to me, although their frowns cleared to be replaced in an instant by determined smiles on the part of my brother and his wife and a wary look on Will's. They were concerned, it appeared, about *me*. The effect on me of what they called the "ordeal" ahead had been the subject of that heads-together discussion. Horrible sights were what they were afraid of, glimpses of the charnel house. One or all of them should go with me. They seemed to believe my life had been sheltered, and perhaps it had been, compared to theirs.

"I shan't be going into the caves," I said as I ordered my breakfast. "It will be some impersonal office with everything spread out and labeled, I expect, like in a museum."

"But you'll be alone."

"Not really. I shall know you're only a few miles away, waiting for me."

The table was bare except for their coffee cups. None of them had eaten a thing. My rolls arrived and butter and jam, my fruit and fruit juice. I suddenly felt unusually hungry.

"Let's see," I said, "what shall we do for the rest of the day? We could take the boat to Formentor for lunch or drive to Lluc. This evening, don't forget, we're having dinner at the Parador de Golondro. Have we booked a table?"

"I'm sorry, Petra, I'm afraid I forgot to do that," Piers said.

"Could you do it while I'm out?" A little fear struck me. I was going to say I don't know why it did, but I do know. "You *will* all be here when I get back, won't you?"

Rosario's voice sounded unlike her. I had never heard bitterness in it before. "Where should we go?"

The car came for me promptly at ten. The driver turned immediately inland and from the road, just before he took the turn for Muralla, I had a sudden bold sight of the *Casita,* glimpsed as it can be between the parting of the hills. It seemed a deeper, brighter color, an ocherish gold, an effect either of new paint or of the sun. But when does the sun not shine? The yellow hills, with their tapestry stitches of gray and dark green, slipped closed again like sliding panels and the house withdrew behind them.

I was right about what awaited me in Muralla, a new office building made of that whitish grainy concrete that has defaced the Mediterranean and is like nothing so much as blocks of cheap ice-cream. Inside, in what I am sure they call the "atrium," was a forest of plastic greenery. There was even a small collection, in Styrofoam amphorae, of plastic strawberry trees. I was led via jungle paths to a room marked *privado* and then and only then, hesitating as two more policemen joined us and a key to the room was produced, did my heart misgive me and a tiny bubble of panic run up to my throat so that I caught my breath.

They were very kind to me. They were big strong macho

men enjoyably occupied in doing what nature had made them for, protecting a woman from the ugliness of life. One of them spoke tolerable English. If I would just look at the things, look at them very carefully, think about what I had seen, and then they would take me away and ask me one or two simple questions. There would be nothing unpleasant. The bones found in the cave—he apologized for their very existence. There was no need for me to see them.

"I would like to see them," I said.

"They cannot be identified after so long."

"I would like to see them."

"Just as you wish," he said, with a shrug, and then the door was opened.

An empty room. A place of drawers and bench tops, like a dissecting room except that all the surfaces were of light polished wood and at the windows hung blinds of pale gray vertical strips. Drawers were opened, trays lifted out and placed on the long central table. I approached it slowly, holding one of my hands clasped in the other and feeling my cold fingertips against my cold damp palm.

Spread before me were two pairs of shoes, the woman's dark blue leather with sling backs and wedge heels, the man's what we call trainers now but "plimsolls" then or "gym shoes"; rags, gnawed by vermin, might once have been a pair of flannel trousers, a shirt, a dress with a tiny pearl button still attached to its collar; a gold chain with pendant cross, a gold watch with bracelet and safety chain, a heavier watch with its leather strap rotted, a child's ring for a little finger, two pinhead turquoises on a gold band thin as wire.

I looked at it all. I looked with indifference but a pretense of care for the sake of those onlookers. The collection of bones was too pitiful to be obscene. Surely this was not all? Perhaps a few specimens only had found their way to this room. I put out my hand and lifted up one of the long bones. The man who had brought me there made a movement toward me but was checked by his superior, who stood there watching me intently. I held the bone in both my hands, feeling its dry worn deadness, gray and grainy, its long-lifeless age, and then I put it down gently.

I turned my back on the things and never looked at them again.

"I have never seen any of this before," I said. "It means nothing to me."

"Are you quite sure? Would you like some time to think about it?"

"No, I am quite sure. I remember very well what my brother and my cousin were wearing."

They listened while I described clothes that Piers and Rosario had had. I enumerated items of jewelry. There was a locket I remembered her wearing the first time we met, a picture of her mother in a gold circlet under a seed pearl lid.

"Thank you very much. You have been most helpful."

"At least I have eliminated a possibility," I said, knowing they would not understand.

They drove me back to Llosar. The fruit on the strawberry trees takes a year to ripen. This year's flowers, blooming now, will become the fruit of twelve months' time. And as soon as it ripens they pick it for making fruit pies. I had this sudden absurd yearning to see those strawberries in the hotel garden again, to see them before the bushes were stripped. I opened the car door myself, got out, and walked up to the hotel without looking back. But instead of going up the steps, I turned aside into the shady garden, the pretty garden of geometric paths and small square pools with yellow fish, the cypresses and junipers gathered in groups as if they had met and stopped to gossip. To the left of me, up in the sun, rose the terrace and beyond it was the swimming pool, but down here grew the arbutus, its white blossom gleaming and its red fruits alight, as shiny as decorations on some northern Christmas tree.

Piers and Rosario were up on the terrace. I am not sure how I knew this, for I was not aware of having looked. I felt their anguished eyes on me; their dread communicated itself to me on the warm, still, expectant air. I knew everything about them, I knew how they felt now. They saw me and read into my action in coming here, in coming immediately to this garden, anger and misery and knowledge of betrayal. Of course, I understood I must put an end to their anguish at once, I must go to them and leave adoration of these sweet-scented snowy flowers and strawberry fruits until another day.

But first I picked one of the fruits and put it in my mouth. Iris Harvey had been wrong. It was not tasteless, it tasted like some fresh crisp vegetable, sharp and strange. It was different, different from any other fruit I had tasted, but not unpleasant. I thought it had the kind of flavor that would grow on me. I walked up the steps to the terrace. Will was nowhere to be seen. With the courage I knew they had, their unconquered brave hearts, they were waiting for me. Decorously, even formally, dressed for that place where the other guests were in swimming costumes, they were nevertheless naked to me, their eyes full of the tragedy of long, wretched, misspent lives. They were holding hands.

"Petra," Piers said. Just my name.

To have kept them longer in suspense would have been the cruelest act of my life. In the time they had been with me I had learned to speak like a human being, like someone who understands love and knows warmth.

"My dears," I said. "How sad you look. There's nothing wrong, is there? I've had such a stupid morning. It was a waste of time going over there. They had nothing to show me but a bundle of rags I've never seen before and some rubbishy jewelry. I don't know what they expected—that all that was something to do with you two?"

They remained there, quite still. I know about the effects of shock. But slowly the joined hands slackened and Rosario withdrew hers. I went up to each of them and kissed them gently. I sat down on the third chair at the table and smiled at them. Then I began to laugh.

"I'm sorry," I said. "I'm only laughing because I'm happy. Children laugh from happiness, so why not us?"

"Why not?" said Piers as if it was a new thought, as if a new world opened before him. "Why not?"

I was remembering how long long ago I had heard my brother ask that same rhetorical question, give that odd form of assent, when Will proposed going into the *Casita* and Rosario had demurred. For a moment I saw us all as we had been, Will in his grass hat, long-legged Rosario with her polished hair, my brother eager with love. I sighed and turned the sigh to a smile.

"Now that's behind me," I said, "we can stay on here and have a holiday. Shall we do that?"

"Why not?" said Piers again, and this time the repetition of those words struck Rosario and me as inordinately funny and we both began to laugh as at some exquisite joke, some example of marvelous wit.

It was thus, convulsed with laughter, that we were found by Will when, having no doubt been watching from some window up above for signs of good or ill, he judged the time right and safe to come out and join us.

"Did you book that table at Golondro?" I said, hoarse with laughter, weak with it.

Will shook his head. I knew he would not have, that none of them would have. "I'll do it this minute," he said.

"Don't be long," I called after him. "We're going to celebrate. I'm going to order a bottle of champagne."

"What are we celebrating, Petra?" said Rosario.

"Oh, just that we're here together again," I said.

They smiled at me for I was bestowing on them, on both of them, the tender look I had never given to any lover. And the feeling that inspired it was better than a lover's glance, being without self-deception, without illusion. Of course, I had never been deceived. I had known, if not quite from the first, from the third day of their appearance, that they were not my brother and his wife. For one thing, a man is not operated on twice in his life for appendicitis. But even without that I would have known. My blood told me and my bones, my thirteen years with a brother I was closer to than to parents or any friend. I knew—always—they were a pair of impostors Will had found and instructed. I knew, almost from the beginning, it was a trick played on me for their gain and Will's.

But there is another way of looking at it. I have bought them and they are mine now. They have to stay, they have nowhere else to go. Isn't that what Piers meant when he said being together was the way it always would be? They are my close companions. We have nothing more to gain from each other, we have made our wills, and the death of one of us will not profit the others.

They have made me happier than I have ever been. I know what people are. I have observed them. I have proved the truth of the recluse's motto, that the onlooker sees most of the game. And I know that Piers and Rosario love me now as I love them, and dislike Will as I dislike him. No doubt they have recompensed him, I don't want to know how, and I foresee a gradual loosening of whatever bond it is that links him to us. It began when I sent him back into the hotel to make that phone call, when Rosario's eyes met mine and Piers pursed his lips in a little moue of doubt.

Am I to end all this with a confrontation, an accusation, casting them out of my life? Am I to retreat—and this time, at my age, finally, for good—into that loneliness that would be even less acceptable than before because now I have seen what else is possible?

I have held my dear brother's bone in my hands. I have seen his clothes that time and decay have turned to rags and touched the ruin of a shoe that once encased his strong slender foot. Now I shall begin the process of forgetting him. I have a new brother and sister to be happy with for the rest of my life.

Will has come back, looking sheepish, not understanding at all what has happened, to tell us we are dining at the Parador de Golondro, the little house of desire, at nine tonight. This is the cue, of course, for some characteristic British complaining about the late hour at which the Spanish dine. Only Rosario has nothing to say, but then she is Spanish herself—or is she?

I resolve never to try to discover this, never to tease, to

lay traps, attempt a catching-out. After all, I have no wish to understand the details of the conspiracy. And when the time comes I will neither listen to nor make deathbed confessions.

For I saw in their eyes just now, as I came to their table to reassure them, that they are no more deceived in me than I am in them. They know that I know and that we all, in our mutual love, can accept.